THE BLOOD OF KINGS

As Frank and Joe were eating, Carlos returned to the back of the bus, his eyes blazing. "There's been an earthquake in Soledad," he said. "I couldn't find out how much damage there was, but they told me it was the biggest in memory. The people are saying it's a sign."

"A sign of what?" Frank asked.

"The god Tsotal," Carlos replied.

Frank let out a low whistle.

"There is more," Carlos said. "According to the legend, the only way to put Tsotal back to sleep is to sacrifice the king of the Ixilans. This will serve Micola's purpose well."

Frank said, "Because your father is a descendant of ancient kings?"

"Yes. He must be the human sacrifice that stops Tsotal from shaking the earth," Carlos concluded.

Books in THE HARDY BOYS CASEFILES™ Series

Available from ARCHWAY Paperbacks

THE HARDY BOYS CASEFILES NO. 101

PEAK OF DANGER

FRANKLIN W. DIXON

AN ARCHWAY PAPERBACK
Published by POCKET BOOKS
New York   London   Toronto   Sydney   Tokyo   Singapore

AN ARCHWAY PAPERBACK *Original*

An Archway Paperback published by
POCKET BOOKS, a division of Simon & Schuster Inc.
1230 Avenue of the Americas, New York, NY 10020

Copyright © 1995 by Simon & Schuster Inc.
Produced by Mega-Books, Inc.

ISBN: 0-671-88212-0

First Archway Paperback printing July 1995

10 9 8 7 6 5 4 3 2 1

THE HARDY BOYS, AN ARCHWAY PAPERBACK
and colophon are registered trademarks of Simon & Schuster Inc.

THE HARDY BOYS CASEFILES is a trademark of
Simon & Schuster Inc.

Cover art by Brian Kotzky

Printed in the U.S.A.

IL 6+

PEAK OF DANGER

Chapter

1

"WHO'S THE NEW KID?" Frank Hardy asked his younger brother, Joe, pointing to a short, stocky guy in bare feet. The kid was wearing soccer shorts and a T-shirt and holding a knapsack. He stood about four feet from Frank and Joe, peering nervously around the locker room.

Joe called over to the new kid, "You look lost."

The boy had to be Native American with his black eyes, black hair, broad forehead, and golden brown skin, Joe decided. He wore his hair in a single braid that hung halfway down his back. In a soft voice with a heavy Spanish accent, he replied, "The freshmen lockers, they are here?" He pointed around a corner toward the back of the locker room.

Coach Jordan isn't going to like that hair, eighteen-year-old Frank mused. He smiled and spoke to the young guy, "You don't have to use the freshmen lockers during summer session. There's plenty of room over here."

Joe added, "Yeah, those old metal lockers will leave rust on your clothes. Use these."

The new kid shook his head. He said, "The man with the uniform, he tells me to place my articles in the freshmen lockers, *solamente.*"

"Suit yourself," Frank said, extending his hand. "My name's Frank Hardy."

"Carlos Capac," returned the young man.

"And I'm Joe Hardy," Joe said, clapping Carlos on the shoulder.

"Hi," Carlos said, then he blushed.

"Hurry up and get dressed," Joe said. "Coach Jordan freaks if you're late for calisthenics."

Carlos disappeared around the corner toward a locker to store his gear as Frank pulled on a Bayport T-shirt, messing up his brown hair. Frank and Joe trotted outside to join the rest of the Bayport High School soccer team for the first day of summer camp. It was a brilliant June morning, and the soccer field had just been mowed.

Coach Jordan seemed to be in a good mood, which Frank thought was lucky, since it was their first day of intensive soccer training camp.

"Everyone here?" Coach Jordan asked. He

was a barrel-chested man with a touch of gray in his hair at the temples and had something of a short fuse. He blew his whistle to gather the team together.

Frank said, "There's a new guy, Coach. Carlos Capac. He'll be out in a second."

Coach Jordan checked his clipboard. "That's right. I got a call about him yesterday. A South American kid, right?"

Just then Carlos trotted out to the group. He wore the regulation Bayport uniform—black satin shorts and bright yellow T-shirt—but he wasn't wearing shin pads or cleats.

"Where are your pads and cleats, kid?" the coach asked.

Carlos looked down at his feet, then at the feet of the other players, who wore regulation shin guards and soccer shoes with rubber cleats. Softly Carlos said, "I don't need them, sir."

The coach's bark ripped through the spring air. "Frank Hardy!"

"Yes, sir!" Frank answered.

"Run and get this kid a pair of shin pads and cleats."

Before Frank could move, Carlos said in a quiet but firm voice, "Please, sir. Truly I do not need the pads or shoes. I am used to playing in bare feet. All the people in my country play this way."

Frank could tell that Coach Jordan was trying

to control his temper, but wasn't doing a very good job of it. "Okay, kid," he said finally. "Go barefoot. But I don't want to hear any complaints later, you hear me?"

"Yes, sir," said Carlos.

The coach ordered the boys to line up in rows to do calisthenics. While they were doing jumping jacks, Joe fired questions at Carlos. "Can you really play better in bare feet?"

"Sure," said Carlos.

"Doesn't it hurt?"

"In my country, soccer shoes are very rare," Carlos said, "and very expensive. So we play in bare feet."

"Where are you from?" Joe continued, brushing his blond hair off his sweaty forehead.

"Payumac," Carlos said. "It's in South America."

"How long have you been here?"

"My parents and I moved to this country two weeks ago."

Frank said, "Aren't the World Cup Soccer Championships being held in Payumac this year?"

"Yes," Carlos said. "They are to start today. I had tickets, but I cannot use them because my parents came here."

"Carlos, my man!" Joe said. "How could you miss the opportunity to see the World Cup?"

Carlos shrugged, but Frank could tell by his frown that it bothered him.

"Couldn't your parents have postponed leaving?" Frank asked. Carlos's angry look surprised Frank, but the newcomer didn't say anything.

Just then Coach Jordan shouted, "Okay, on your backs. Give me a hundred sit-ups."

While he was doing his crunches, Frank made a mental note—the kid was hiding something. He resolved to find out what it was before the day was done, but there wasn't much chance to talk later. Drill work took a lot of concentration, with Coach Jordan pairing off players to practice blocking maneuvers.

During the blocking drills, Joe took a few kicks because he was constantly distracted by watching Carlos's awesome footwork. Carlos was quick on his feet and very skillful.

It wasn't until the scrimmage that Carlos really showed Frank and Joe what a superior player he was, though. Joe played left wing for the Skins, so he pulled his shirt off over his head. Carlos was assigned to play right wing for the Shirts, so he left his shirt on. Joe knew that he would be ghosting Carlos for the entire game as the ball passed down the field. Frank was goalie for the Skins.

The boys trotted into position to wait for the kickoff. Coach Jordan tossed the ball into play. The Skins took possession immediately, but the ball was soon passed over to the Shirts. As the game progressed—with the ball changing sides frequently—Joe found that Carlos could run circles around him. The guy was short, but he could move like the wind, and his feet attracted the ball as if he had magnets in his toes.

Joe knew that he was no match for Carlos, and each time the new player stole the ball from him his frustration grew. He noticed that the young South American was a careful player, never fouling, tripping, or pushing. Joe respected Carlos's by-the-book technique, but he also knew that such cautious playing had a built-in disadvantage. During a break when substitutions were being made, Joe told the rest of the Skins, "Let's set up a pick on Carlos."

His friend Tony Prito grinned. "That's a tough move, pal. Don't you want to take it a little easy on our first day of practice?"

"What's the matter?" Joe said to his wiry, dark-haired friend. "Can't you handle it?"

"Sure I can," Tony affirmed.

When the Skins had possession of the ball, Joe received a pass from Tony, then dribbled down the field toward the Shirts' goal. He maneuvered the ball toward the sideline, careful not to let it pass out-of-bounds.

As Joe expected, Carlos ran along beside him. The setup was perfect for a pick. Tony swooped into position behind Joe. Keeping a keen eye on the ball, Joe executed a reverse pass by stepping deftly in front of the rolling ball and then kicking

it backward with his heel. What Joe hadn't antici-
pated was how quickly Carlos could reverse direction, or how lightning fast he could block a
pass.

The South American player was gone before
Joe could take two steps, and with him went the
ball. Carlos passed it to his left wing guard. By
the time Joe caught up to him, the Shirts had
dribbled the ball down to where Frank was preparing to defend the Skins' goal.

Carlos glanced over at Joe and held his hand
up for an imaginary high five. Joe couldn't help
grinning. "Awesome move, Carlos," he shouted,
even though Carlos had just stolen the ball
from him.

Coach Jordan's whistle pierced the air at the
end of the game. The scrimmage ended in defeat
for Frank and Joe's team. The Shirts beat them
three to two—Carlos scoring all three Shirt goals.
"Great soccer, boys," the coach shouted. When
the two teams had gathered around him at mid-
field, he clapped Carlos on the shoulder, saying,
"Good to have you with us, kid. Hit the
showers!"

Inside the locker room the noise level was at
an all-time high as the team got ready to leave.

As Frank and Joe were drying off after their
showers, Frank said, "It looks like our newest
player is going to be our best."

"No kidding," Joe replied. Just then Carlos

passed them on the way to his locker. "Hey, Carlos," Joe called out. "You want to show me some of that barefoot magic this afternoon? I have a feeling you'll be able to teach me something."

"No problem, *amigo,*" said the dark-eyed youth, peeling off his yellow T-shirt. "I'll wait for you outside."

After he disappeared around the corner, Joe leaned over to Frank. "Did you see that tattoo?"

Frank nodded. He'd been surprised to see the band of geometric designs inked into Carlos's upper arm. "It looks like some kind of Native American symbol," he said.

"I wonder if it hurt when he got it."

Frank was about to answer when he heard a loud *pffsst!* and the lights above his head dimmed. In the sudden silence that fell, all fourteen boys gazed up at the ceiling. The quiet was shattered by a sharp yelp from the bank of lockers around the corner. The air crackled with electricity, and the lights flickered on and off. Joe was the first to duck around the corner, and what he saw made his stomach twist.

Carlos was on the floor, moaning, while a live electrical cable twisted like a dancing snake near his head, showering sparks and smoke every time it brushed the floor.

Chapter

2

"STAND BACK!" FRANK shouted, rushing past Joe to kneel beside Carlos.

Joe backed away from the end of the swinging cable that was brushing the wet floor beside the lockers. The guys from the team tried to crowd in close, but Joe held them back.

"Any way to cut off the power?" Joe asked. Carlos was starting to move, and Joe could see that his head was close enough to the cable to get hit by it as it twisted randomly. The sparks showering from the blackened tip were as bright as a spot welder's torch, and Joe could smell the acrid smoke of the electrical short circuit.

Frank quickly traced the wire up the wall to where it was dangling from a circuit breaker box.

He reached for the emergency shutoff lever, yanking it down to the Off position. The entire locker room fell into darkness—the electricity was off except for that feeding the live sparking cable, which continued to dance. Frantically Frank searched for the main power box. Luckily it had been placed inside and only a few feet from the circuit breaker. He shut it off. The buzzing, sparking cable instantly stopped moving and became silent. The dim glow from the emergency exit sign was all that illuminated Carlos's body. He was trying to sit up, but there was something wrong with his shoulder.

"One of you guys go get help. We need medical assistance," Frank said.

Joe glanced behind him and saw Tony. "Run and get Coach Jordan in here pronto. And get someone to call nine-one-one—okay?"

"Gotcha," said Tony, who turned to sprint outside.

Kneeling at Carlos's side, Frank felt the young man's forehead, which was cool and waxy, then he placed his ear to Carlos's chest. "His vital signs aren't good," Frank told Joe. "Heart rate is high, shallow breathing, cold sweat, fluttering eyelids." A couple of months earlier, he and Joe had taken an advanced EMS training course, but he never dreamed he'd have to use the knowledge so soon.

Just then Coach Jordan arrived. "Okay, break

this up." The rest of the team scattered, falling back as the coach approached. "What's the problem, boys?"

"An electrical short," Frank said. "Looks like he got a pretty big jolt."

By now Carlos was fully awake. He started to sit up, but Joe gently held him down, saying, "Not yet, buddy. Just relax. You're going to be okay. EMS will be here any minute."

"*¿Qué pasa?*" he murmured. He looked around him, wincing as he tried to move his arm.

"I think the shoulder's dislocated," Joe said.

As if on cue, the piercing wail of sirens filled the locker room. Frank breathed a heavy sigh of relief.

"Take over here," he told Joe.

While Joe stayed close to Carlos, Frank inspected the damaged wire closely. It had been pulled loose right at the point where the edge of a locker met the wall. The end of the wire resembled a head of cauliflower—a melted mass of plastic and shredded wire. Looking at the edge of the locker, Frank noticed a short tab of metal that had fastened the locker to the wall. It had been bent so that it bit into the wire. He checked the other metal tabs above and below the bent one. All were properly fastened to the wall. For only a few seconds Frank wondered why the tab, so close to the cable, had been bent. Somebody bent it, he thought to himself, because somebody wanted it to look like an accident. It was a clever piece of work.

"Look at the floor," Joe said. "Carlos was standing in a huge puddle."

"That's why he got such a big jolt," Frank said. Lowering his voice and pulling Joe off to one side, he whispered, "I doubt this was an accident." He showed Joe the bent metal tab on the locker.

Joe's eyes traveled down the edge of the locker. On the floor he noticed some brightly colored bits of plastic. He bent to pick them up. They were tiny bits of wire insulation, curled like wood shavings from a carpenter's plane. "Oh, no," Joe said. "Look what I found."

"That's enough for me," Frank said, studying the shavings. "Those have obviously been whittled away from the cable. Looks like we've got ourselves a clear-cut case of sabotage."

Their conference was interrupted by the arrival of the paramedics, who were wheeling in a gurney. Frank and Joe watched as the man and woman strapped Carlos onto it. Joe agreed to ride in the ambulance with Carlos and stay with him.

"I'll stick around to see what else I can find," Frank said.

By the time the ambulance left, Coach Jordan had sent everyone but Frank home. Frank followed Coach Jordan into his office, a small room littered with stacks of paper, dusty trophies, broken sports equipment, and a state-of-the-art security system.

"I'm really going to let building maintenance have it. That kid could have been killed. Why those wires aren't buried in the wall I'll never know."

"Yeah. And look at the accident they caused." Frank didn't really believe what had happened was an accident, but he wanted to see Coach Jordan's reaction.

"Accident my foot," Coach Jordan said. "An electrician came around at eight this morning, just when I was opening up, saying he had to check for some possible code violations."

"What electrician?" Frank asked.

"I don't know. Some inspector type in a uniform."

"He didn't leave his card or say the name of his company?" Frank pressed.

"No." Coach Jordan scrutinized Frank's face. "What are you getting at? Are you saying that electrician had something to do with what happened to Carlos?"

"I don't know, but I'd like to make sure he didn't. We've got to watch out for our new MVP, right?"

Coach Jordan nodded, smiling. "He's good. And even without any shoes." He smiled more broadly, then sighed. "Okay, the electrician, let me see. I've got it—he said he was hired by the

13

school. He had a Spanish accent, and was wearing dark gray coveralls. He had a mustache, I think."

"What did he say?"

"Just that he needed to look around the locker room. I let him in and went into my office to figure out the workout schedule for this week. Which reminds me, I have to finish up a bit of work here and then get over to the hospital."

"I guess that's my signal to take off. I'll just look around a little more," Frank said.

"Be my guest," Coach Jordan said. "I'll have to leave soon."

Frank returned to the locker room. Wondering why the circuit breaker hadn't blown the first time the severed wire made contact with the floor, Frank opened the circuit breaker box and flipped all the other switches to the On position after isolating the severed wire's connection. Light flooded the locker room. Then he noticed it—the shunt, a small length of wire attached to the cut wire that allowed the cable to bypass the circuit breaker. The only way to stop electricity flowing through it was to throw the main power switch as he had. This was no accident.

"Find anything?" asked the coach from behind Frank.

"Nah," Frank lied. "Except, of course, the severed wire will have to be fixed."

"Great," said Jordan. "That's another thing I'll have to tell the principal. She wants a full report on the incident. I'm going over to her house after the hospital."

On a hunch Frank asked, "Say, Coach, did you tell Carlos to use the freshmen lockers?"

"I didn't see him till he came out on the field." Coach Jordan chuckled. "Believe me, if I'd seen him *before* practice I would have said something about that hair!"

"Want me to lock up when I'm done here?" Frank asked.

Coach Jordan said, "Great, and don't forget to check the security system."

"Okay," Frank said. He examined the locker room one last time but didn't find any more clues. Before leaving, he remembered to check the security system in the coach's office. It had been installed after some vandals had broken into the gym and spray-painted graffiti all over the walls. All the TV monitors except one were working fine. Each one showed a different view— one of the basketball court, swimming pool, and soccer field. A sign under the blank screen said Locker Room.

Frank pushed the Rewind button, waited for a few seconds, then pushed Play. On the black-and-white TV screen, he saw several seconds of tape of himself, along with Joe, Carlos, and the rest of the team suiting up for practice. Next he saw the camera pointed toward the freshmen lockers. Perfect shot, he said to himself.

Frank rewound the tape again. The next shot was of a mustached man wearing coveralls and carrying a step ladder and tool box coming into view at the bottom of the screen. He set up the ladder and climbed it, disappearing under the camera lens. Then without warning his face filled the screen. He squinted at something behind the camera. His hand flashed across the snowy TV screen, holding a pair of pliers. He gave a little grin as if to say, "So long, suckers." Then the camera went blank.

Frank thought he should take the tape with him. It contained valuable evidence, and this was probably the man who had fixed the cable to short out. As he stood deciding whether or not to take the tape, he heard the door leading out to the playing fields click shut. It was a tiny sound, but it registered in Frank's brain like a fire siren. He crept out of the office, not wanting to be trapped in there, and dove behind a laundry bin, peeking up over the edge.

The mustached man wandered in, carrying his ladder. First he went to the freshmen lockers where the wire had torn loose from the wall. Let me guess, Frank thought to himself. He's going to fix the metal tab so that no one will suspect sabotage.

The man did set up the ladder and climb up to the camera, where he reconnected the wires so the camera would work again. As the electrician stepped down, Frank noticed something that made his heart stop. Around the electrician's waist was a tool belt, and dangling from it was a knife sheathed in a leather case—a hunting knife, judging by the handle. Why would an electrician need a knife like that? Frank wondered.

As soon as the door clicked shut behind the man, Frank was up and moving into the coach's office. He paused only to eject the tape from the machine, then cracked the door to peer out. No sign of the electrician. He moved across the floor and slipped out into the afternoon sunshine, hugging the wall of the gym on his way to the parking lot.

As Frank rounded the corner of the gym, he stopped short with a sharp intake of breath. The electrician was kneeling right in front of him, tying his shoe. The man glanced up, equally surprised, then his eyes narrowed suspiciously.

"Where did you come from?" he asked in a growl thick with a Spanish accent. He stood up and was taller than Frank. His hand went for the handle of his knife.

Chapter

3

THINKING FAST, Frank held up the VHS tape. "I came from the library. I got this tape."

The electrician held Frank in his steely gaze, his fingers twitching on the handle of his knife, his dark eyes glinting. "Are you sure about that?" he asked in his thick Spanish accent.

Frank glanced at the tape and was horrified to see the words *Security—Do Not Remove* printed boldly on the side. "This?" he said. "It's, um, a security tape. I'm on the student security team here at Bayport High, and there have been some problems lately with vandalism. We're trying to stop it." His voice grew more confident, more authoritative. "Say, who are you, anyway? Do you have any identification?"

The electrician hadn't expected this and was momentarily confused. "I am just an electrician—"

"Security cards are issued to all outside contractors," Frank interrupted. "Where's yours?"

"My partner's got it," the electrician growled, clearly growing agitated. Frank wondered if he'd gone too far. The man's eyes were shifting nervously, and his hand was wrapped around the knife handle now.

"Well, you should carry your ID at all times," Frank said, starting to move on. The electrician didn't move. "But I'll let it slide this time."

Frank continued on down the sidewalk toward the parking lot. With each step, he expected to be attacked from behind. When he finally did dare to look back, the electrician was gone.

Joe said goodbye to the coach, shivering in his short-sleeved T-shirt. He hunched up his shoulders in a futile attempt to stay warm. The hospital emergency room was chillier than an ice box, and the antiseptic smell made him feel slightly queasy. He wished the doctor would hurry up with Carlos's examination.

The doctor finally did shove aside the white curtain that divided Carlos's bed from the three others in the room. The doctor was a prim woman in her middle fifties, wearing a white smock and glasses. Joe had overheard most of what she'd said to Carlos and knew he was going to be all right. His shoulder was sprained, and he'd have to wear a sling for a few days while it healed.

"Right now," the doctor was saying, "I want you to stick around for two more hours, just to make sure your heart rate remains steady. Electrical shocks can interfere with your body's own pulse. I doubt you'll have any complications, but I want to make sure. I wish we could reach your parents—they should be notified."

"They cannot be disturbed, and I am well," Carlos said. "But I will remain here as you request."

Joe stood up and introduced himself. "Will Carlos be able to play soccer soon?"

The doctor smiled. "Sure," she said. "Sooner than you'd think." She made a few last notes on Carlos's chart and then walked out into the hallway.

Carlos grinned after the doctor had left. "The lady doctor is good, no?"

"*Sí*," said Joe. "First-rate, but she's way too old for you, buddy," Joe said, laughing. "If you're looking for a girlfriend, I might be able to help you out. Are you staying in Bayport long?"

Carlos's smile wavered just a little bit. "Sure," he said.

"You don't sound convinced," Joe replied.

"I am playing on the soccer team, am I not?" Carlos said defensively.

"Well, yes," Joe said. Gesturing at the sling, he added, "I mean, eventually."

Carlos scowled, lifting up his arm. "This? By tomorrow I will be feeling much better. You will see. I will meet you on the field in two days to show you barefoot soccer playing."

"Carlos," Joe said. "You've got to level with me. This wasn't any accident. Somebody is out to hurt you." When Carlos didn't respond, Joe continued, "Frank and I think somebody fixed the wires deliberately so you'd get hurt—maybe even killed. Can you think of anyone who'd want to harm you?"

Carlos was startled. "Why do you think it was not an accident?"

Joe told him about the wire shavings and the bent metal tab. "It's definitely a professional job," he concluded, "and we've got to notify the police."

Carlos's troubled expression grew more serious. "No. No police. You must promise this. No police." He started biting on a fingernail, his eyes darting back and forth. "I must get out of here," he said finally.

"Why?" Joe asked, concerned. "What's the matter?"

Carlos threw off the hospital sheet and swung his legs over the side of the bed. "It does not concern you." He spotted the telephone beside his bed and snatched up the receiver. "Please," he said. "I would like some privacy. I must make a call to my parents."

"But I thought your parents couldn't be—" Joe started to say.

At that moment Frank appeared in the doorway. Joe was relieved to see him and joined Frank in the hall outside. Joe's expression revealed his frustration. "I can't get anything out of him, but something's definitely wrong. As soon as he heard about the sabotage, he became agitated and anxious to leave. He wouldn't tell me who could have done it or why."

"I met the guy who tampered with the wires. And I have proof."

"Who was he?" Joe asked.

"I don't know," Frank replied. "But he's on tape. This guy took the trouble to cover his tracks—or tried to."

"Maybe if we show the tape to Carlos, he'll open up, as long as he understands we really want to help him." Joe took the tape from Frank. "I'll make a copy," he said.

The boys' van had been torched on their last case. Luckily their insurance had paid most of the cost to replace it with an almost identical van loaded with even more gadgets and state-of-the-art tracking and detecting devices. These included a new laptop computer.

"Where is the van?"

"Just outside the entrance, to the right."

"Keep an eye on Carlos." Without further explanation, Joe walked down the hallway, past the nurse's station and waiting room, and through the automatic glass doors of the emergency room entrance.

Frank peered into Carlos's room. He was still on the telephone, his back to the doorway, listening intently. Frank decided Carlos would be occupied a bit longer and decided to find a soda machine. He wandered out to the waiting room and started past the sliding glass doors to the outside.

As he passed in front of the doors, they sprang open. After Frank located the electric eye above the doors, he glanced outside to the street, where the traffic was backed up because a commercial van was trying to squeeze into a small parking spot across the street. It was an old van, with the words *Electro-Wizard* painted on the side. Frank recognized the lightning bolt logo; he had seen other Electro-Wizard vans around town.

Pulling change from his pocket, Frank approached the soda machine. Just as he was about to make a selection, he heard the nurse shout, "Hey! Wait! You can't leave!" The sliding glass doors opened with a whoosh, and Frank just had time to see the blur of Carlos flying through them, his injured arm tucked close to his side.

"Hey, Carlos!" Frank shouted, and sprinted through the glass doors and out onto the sidewalk. He looked to his right, then to his left and saw Carlos running quickly down the sidewalk.

At the same time Frank heard the screech of tires. The Electro-Wizard van across the street was moving quickly into traffic in the direction Carlos was running. As the van passed by Frank, he got a glimpse of the driver—mustache, dark hair. The electrician. Frank raced over to the curb about twenty feet away where his van was parked.

Joe was in the back with the laptop computer out. "Hey, Frank," he said. "I was just—"

"Carlos is in big trouble!" Frank shouted, and powered up the van. He made a quick U-turn in order to follow Carlos and the Electro-Wizard van.

Steadying himself as the van turned, Joe shut down the laptop and returned it to its compartment in the back. He'd been able to print a copy of an image of the electrician from the videotape, using the camcorder to record several seconds of tape into their new CD-ROM laptop computer. He snatched the paper copy from the portable printer and crawled forward to join Frank. Buckling into the passenger seat, he said, "Where is he? What happened back there?"

"The Electro-Wizard van up ahead is chasing him," Frank said.

As Joe spotted the van about half a block ahead, its brake lights lit up, and it skidded sideways, barely making a tight turn into an alleyway at the edge of the hospital building.

Frank stepped on the gas, and when they reached the corner of the alley he didn't slow down to turn into it.

"Frank!" Joe shouted, watching in horror as they shot past the alleyway. "What are you doing?"

"This alley leads to the hospital Dumpsters. It's curved and connects to Main Street just around the corner. I'm betting we'll intercept Carlos there."

Joe fixed his eyes on the approaching corner of Main Street. "If he doesn't make it, we're going to end up with one dead soccer player after all."

Chapter

4

THE HARDYS' VAN SKITTERED around the corner onto Main Street, then rocketed toward the end of the alley. Joe saw nothing at first. Then all at once Carlos flew out of the alley with the electrician's truck close behind.

Carlos dodged right as soon as he hit the sidewalk, escaping the Electro-Wizard's grillwork by just a few feet. The truck banked and turned as the driver slammed on the brakes.

Frank maneuvered around the Electro-Wizard truck as it skidded sideways across Main Street, bouncing up against the far curb. As they shot past it, Frank said, "Get ready to pick up Carlos." He slowed as he pulled abreast of the sprinting soccer player.

Joe unbuckled his seat belt and leapt in the back, opening the rear door. When he saw Carlos, he called out, "Yo, Carlos! Want a ride?"

One look was all Carlos needed. Without breaking stride, he stepped into the street and leapt up into the still-moving van. Joe pulled the door shut, whooping and shouting. "We caught us a big one, Frank. Let's move!"

"You got it," Frank said, his eyes on the rearview mirror. The Electro-Wizard van was not far behind them. Frank didn't know how much power it had under its hood, but he doubted it could match the eight-cylinder torque machine that powered this van. He pressed the pedal to the metal and felt a surge as the engine shifted into overdrive.

Carlos fell backward into the swivel chair that was bolted to the floor behind the driver's seat. Joe grinned as he braced himself against the rocking of the van. "Better buckle your seat belt, pal."

He deftly slid into his own seat up front, checking out his sideview mirror for their pursuer.

Frank knew this neighborhood pretty well, and in his head he had already mapped out an escape route. Behind the hospital was a section of town comprised of abandoned warehouses, open lots, and a couple of desolate parking lots. Not someplace anyone would take a date, but a good place to lose a renegade electrician in what he suspected was a stolen truck.

Frank took two corners at thirty-five miles an hour, feeling the van strain. It fishtailed wildly, then responded to the straightaway with phenomenal power.

Their pursuers were no match for the Hardys, and the boys soon lost them. "Looks like the Electro-Wizard lost his magic," Frank mused. He circled back to cruise by the hospital a few minutes later. There was no Electro-Wizard van in sight.

"That doctor isn't going to be very happy about your sudden departure, Carlos," Joe remarked, "Don't you think we should go back and apologize to her?"

Carlos was still breathing hard, but he managed to say, "No. You must take me home immediately."

Joe whirled around in his seat. "Look, pal," he said. "Either you drop your attitude, or we're going to drop you off right here."

"Relax," Frank said. "Both of you." To Carlos he said, "We'll take you home. Where do you live?"

"It's over by the expressway," he said. "By the entrance ramp."

"But there aren't any houses over there," Frank said. "Just gas stations, fast food, and—"

"And a motel," Carlos finished for him. "That

is where we are staying. My parents are looking for a place to live."

"It'll take fifteen minutes," Frank said. Checking his rearview mirror, he added, "That is, if we don't have to make any unscheduled detours."

Joe was fuming. He couldn't understand why Carlos was being so ungrateful for all the help he and Frank had given him. Frank noticed that Carlos, too, was agitated.

"Can't you tell us what's happening?" Joe asked grudgingly.

Carlos's face was stony, but his intense black eyes glittered fiercely under his dark eyebrows. His eyes seemed to caution Joe against questioning him. "You would not understand," Carlos said finally.

"It's cool," Frank said. "You don't have to tell us anything you don't want to."

Pulling the laser printout out of his pocket and handing it to Carlos, Joe said, "Do you recognize this guy?"

"We have reason to believe he's the one who arranged the electrical jolt that put you in the hospital," Frank added.

Carlos took the page, unfolded it, and glanced at the photograph. His eyes widened briefly, then narrowed.

"Well?" Joe demanded. "Do you know him or not?"

Carlos's eyes rested briefly on Joe's face as if

he were deciding something. Making up his mind, he took a deep breath and spoke. "I am grateful for your assistance. But there is so much to say. I am not easy with your language. And it is not my way to tell private things to strangers."

Joe relaxed. Now they were getting somewhere. "Hey, look, we're not strangers. We play on the same soccer team, right? We promised to learn from each other."

"Very well," Carlos said. He took another deep breath. "My father has been kidnapped. I only just learned of this when I called my mother. This is why I had to leave the hospital."

"Kidnapped?" Joe said.

"Yes," said Carlos. "This morning." His voice got hard and flat, and he balled his hands into fists. Through gritted teeth he said, "They tied him like a pig and told my mother that I had been killed."

"Brutal," Joe said. Carlos's attitude began to make some sense. "I'll bet it's the same folks who are after you. Who are they?"

"*Los lobos blancos,*" Carlos said. "The White Wolves. It's here in this picture."

"Let me see that," Joe said. The photo showed the electrician's face, with his mustache and dark eyes. Part of his hand appeared at the bottom of the page, close up to the camera and slightly out of focus. On his third finger was a large ring with some kind of insignia on it. "Is that a wolf's head?" Joe asked.

"Yes," said Carlos. "It is the symbol for the military police in my country. They have followed my family here to the U.S."

"Why?" Frank asked.

"It is my father," Carlos answered. "He is much respected by my people—they call him el señor Capac. He hopes to become elected president of our country. The elections are only one month away. The campaign has been difficult because his opposition is Enrique Micola, the current dictator of our country."

"Then why did you come to the U.S.?" Joe asked.

"They tried to kill my father two weeks ago in Telos by planting a bomb under his car. But the bomb malfunctioned, exploding when no one was around. No casualties, but part of our school was damaged." Carlos paused, then explained, "My father runs a school in Telos called Instituto de la Paz, or 'The Peace Institute.' I am a student there." Carlos's face fell. "That is, I used to be a student there."

Frank said, "I've heard about this Micola guy. He was the one who invited the World Soccer Cup Championships to be in your country this year."

"Yes," Carlos said. "For the first time he has opened up our country to the outside world. But he is a liar and a killer. Inviting the World Cup Soccer Championships to be in Payumac is just to persuade other countries that he is a benevolent leader. Nobody in my country trusts him, and everyone fears *los lobos,* the military police."

"But he is allowing democratic elections this year, isn't he?" Frank asked. "Didn't the U.S. put pressure on him?"

"Yes," Carlos said. "I am impressed with your knowledge of our tiny country. Most people do not know it exists. For the first time in twenty years, Micola agreed to elections. My father is the only Ixilan candidate, and this makes him a threat to Micola. Especially near our family's hometown, Soledad. But now my father's dreams for freedom will come to nothing."

Frank said, "We studied Payumac in geography class. It's on the west coast of South America, right? It's the home of the ancient tribe of Ixilans."

"I am Ixilan," Carlos announced proudly. "My ancestors were the kings."

"Wow," Joe said. "That makes you a prince."

Carlos flashed a rare smile. "Technically, yes. But we are no longer a powerful people. We are now a poor people living in the mountains. I hope you can visit Soledad some day. It is near El Gigante, a dormant volcano."

"If your father gets elected president, it would

be like your ancestors coming back into power again—only in the modern world."

Carlos answered dismally. "That will never happen. Micola will not allow it."

Joe fell into deep thought. He felt sorry for Carlos, whose life had been turned upside down. In a low voice, he said, "Listen, Carlos, we'll help you find your dad. This Micola guy has got to learn a lesson about our country. He can't just come here and kidnap people."

"Thank you for your offer of help," Carlos said, "but my problems are not yours. I will find my father. I only hope he is alive when I do."

"But we could start by contacting the local police," Joe said. "Frank and I have friends down at the station—"

"There's your motel," Frank interrupted. "If we want to talk to the police, they're already here."

"Good," Joe said. "Maybe they have some news about your dad." To himself, he added, I only hope the news is good.

Chapter

5

THE MOTEL WAS a two-story building, with rows of doors on the first and second floors facing the parking lot. A Bayport police cruiser was parked in front.

Frank followed Carlos and Joe into one motel room as soon as he parked the van. The first person he noticed was Chief Ezra Collig standing between the two beds. Collig nodded at Frank and Joe, but didn't say anything. He was holding a pad of paper and writing on it.

Carlos's mother sat on the edge of one of the two beds, her face streaked with tears. A flick of her eyes showed she noticed Frank and Joe but immediately she returned her gaze to her son.

Carlos knelt at her feet, holding one of her

hands and peering into her face. He asked a question in Spanish, then another. She answered quietly, her voice shaking with emotion.

Señora Capac had the striking features of the Ixilan. Like her son, she had coppery brown skin, a broad forehead, oval face, and dark eyes. Her long, straight, raven black hair was braided in two plaits, the ends of which were tied in a loose knot halfway down her back. She was dressed in traditional Ixilan garb, a long skirt with multi-colored patterns in red, yellow, and black. Frank noticed the fabric bore the same geometric pattern he'd seen tattooed on Carlos's upper arm.

Chief Collig finished what he was writing before turning to Frank and Joe. "I suppose this young man is a friend of yours."

Frank was about to answer yes when Joe jumped in. "Chief, you're looking great. Have you been lifting weights or something?"

Collig smoothed his hands over the front of his shirt. "It's just a bullet-proof vest. New regulations say we have to wear them on all field calls." Suddenly realizing he'd been sidetracked, he said, "Look, do either of you boys know Spanish? I sent my backup to pick up a translator, but she hasn't returned yet. This lady doesn't speak English. I think Mrs. Capac's husband's missing or something."

"Kidnapped," Carlos said in a low voice. He was still looking at his mother, holding her hand.

"Did you say kidnapped?" Chief Collig asked.

"That's right," Joe said. "Chief Collig, Carlos Capac." Carlos stood and shook hands with the chief.

"What happened to your arm?" Collig asked.

"An accident during soccer practice," Carlos answered.

Frank cleared his throat and met Carlos's eye. He didn't like keeping things from Chief Collig. "You'd better tell him everything," he said. "You can trust him."

The young Ixilan glanced nervously at Chief Collig, then back at Frank. "Very well," he said. "It was no accident. Somebody is trying to kill me."

"We have reason to believe that it's an international problem," Joe added.

Chief Collig leaned up against the bureau. "Somehow that doesn't surprise me," he said sardonically. "But maybe we should start with your father, Carlos. When did you last see him?"

"This morning."

"How did you learn he was missing?"

Carlos glanced at his mother. "She told me on the telephone."

"What did she say happened?"

Fighting for control, Carlos said, "They broke into the room. They tied him up and frightened my mother. Then they took him away."

"Did she know the assailants?"

Carlos translated the question, then replied after his mother's answer. "She says no, but she knows who sent them."

"How does she know that?"

"There was a note," Carlos replied.

"Let's see it," Chief Collig said. Carlos asked his mother in Spanish, and she produced a crumpled piece of stationery. Carlos handed it to the chief.

"Can you translate this?" Chief Collig asked, looking over the paper.

Carlos nodded and gazed at the paper. "It says, 'Tsotal is waking up. The king of the Ixilans must die in the *fuego del Gigante*'—that is the name of a volcano in my country. And then it says, '*¡Viva Enrique Micola!*'—long live Micola."

"Micola is the president of Payumac," Frank explained.

"The note must be written by his supporters," Carlos added. "My father is running for president against Micola. Or he was. This note says that he may be dead."

Frank studied the note carefully. "Actually, it says your father '*must* die,' right? Wouldn't that mean it hasn't happened yet?"

Carlos smiled ruefully. "You don't know Micola. When he says somebody must die, they die."

"I'm afraid this situation is out of my jurisdiction," Chief Collig said. "I'm going to have to call in the FBI. They handle international terrorism cases." He picked up the telephone receiver and dialed. "Patch me through to the federal desk, would you please?"

While Collig was on the telephone, Frank and Joe went up to Señora Capac and sat on either side of her. With her son translating, she said it was an honor to meet them, and if circumstances were better she would offer them refreshments.

"Actually," Joe said, "I could go for a soda right about now. There must be a machine in the lobby. Anybody else?"

"Sure," said Frank. "We may be here awhile."

While Joe went to get some cans of soda, Frank and Carlos puzzled over the kidnapper's note. Carlos explained that Tsotal was the name for one of the gods of ancient Ixilan myth, the god of volcanos. "My father told me all of our myths. Of course we cannot take these stories literally, but they are important because they teach us about our past."

"What's the myth about Tsotal?" Frank asked.

Carlos screwed up his forehead. "Tsotal is an evil god who was lulled into an eternal sleep by a sorcerer. He sleeps in the center of the volcano. Every now and then he wakes up. And when he does, he shakes the earth until he is put back to sleep."

Frank was surprised when Carlos began to smile. "My father told me that Ixilans have learned to walk softly on the earth because we're afraid of waking up Tsotal."

Frank said, "That may explain why you're such an awesome soccer player, but it doesn't explain this note. I mean, why mention this ancient myth in connection with your dad's kidnapping?"

"I don't know."

"Maybe your mom has some ideas." While Carlos questioned his mother, Frank glanced over at Chief Collig. He was speaking to someone at the FBI.

"They're citizens of Payumac. They have visas, so somebody down at the State Department must have heard of them. That's right—kidnapped. What? Bring them where? The consulate in New York City? Do you think I have nothing better to do than—" He listened to the person on the other end of the line. "Fine," he said. "Yes, I see. Well, if you put it that way, okay."

He hung up the phone and stood up. "Mrs. Capac, my instructions are to take you and your son to the Payumac consulate in New York. You'll probably want to pack some things, and then we can be on our way."

Carlos translated rapidly into Spanish, and his mother shook her head vehemently. Carlos explained that his father had warned them that the Payumac consulate in New York City was dangerous.

Frank could tell Collig wasn't pleased with this

resistance. Thinking quickly, Frank interrupted. "You know, Chief, Joe and I could take them in our van if you have to do something more important. Let me call my dad to ask permission."

Chief Collig actually looked as if he would consider the idea, but then he shook his head. "Thanks, but, no, I have to do it myself."

Just then the phone rang. Chief Collig glanced at Señora Capac, who had reacted with alarm. After taking a moment to regain her composure, she answered and quickly motioned to Frank, *"Tu hermano,"* she said, meaning "your brother."

Joe was on the phone. "Our friend in the Electro-Wizard van is back, and he's got a buddy with him. They're parked across the lot," he told Frank.

Frank's stomach sank. Carrying the phone across the bed to the window, he peeked outside, careful to conceal himself behind the drapes. He scanned the parking lot. About fifty yards away, parked in clear view of the motel room, was the van. "I see them," he whispered. "Where are you?"

"In the lobby, off to your right," Joe said.

Frank swiveled around. "I can't see you. You okay?"

"I'm safe for now," Joe said. "But one more thing. I think I saw a gun."

"Okay, little brother," Frank said. "It's time for us to do a little fancy footwork."

"They wouldn't do anything with Collig here, would they?" Joe asked.

"I wouldn't put it past them," Frank said.

"So what do we do?"

"Can you make it to the van?" Frank asked.

"Probably," Joe said. "But once they see me getting into the van, they'll know I'm with Carlos and come after me."

Frank said, "Stay where you are then, and stay on the line. Let me check with the others." He glanced behind him. Carlos, Señora Capac, and Chief Collig were all staring at him. "It looks like there's a bit of trouble outside," he said. "Our friends in the van are back."

Carlos jumped up to look out the window. He began speaking rapidly to his mother. Meanwhile, Frank dropped the phone on the bed and went into the bathroom, where there was a window. It was a small space, but he thought he could squeeze through. Carlos, too, but not Señora Capac, and certainly not Chief Collig.

The chief was right behind him. "What's going on?"

"Remember we told you that someone tried to kill Carlos?" Frank said in a deadly serious voice. Chief Collig nodded. "Well, the man who did it is back with a friend." Without waiting for a response, Frank went back to the phone. "Joe," he

41

said. "I'm going out through the bathroom window. If the men in that truck move, you'll have to distract them."

"Great," Joe said. "Any idea how?"

"You'll figure it out," Frank replied. "I'll join you in a second."

After Frank hung up, Chief Collig grabbed his arm.

"Look, I've had about enough of this," he said. "You're not going to crawl out of any bathroom window until I know why."

"Chief, there isn't time," Frank said urgently. "Those guys mean business."

"Oh, really?" said the chief. "We'll just see about that." He whirled around and reached for the door.

Frank said, "Wait, Chief! They might have a—"

Too late. Before he could say the word *gun,* the sharp rattle of a submachine gun interrupted him. The bullets splintered the wooden door frame. Chief Collig spun around in the doorway and fell to the floor.

Chapter

6

FRANK WAS SURE Chief Collig was dead. He had seen the bullet hit, ripping a hole right in the center of the man's chest.

Frank ran over to him and quickly pulled him out of the doorway and back into the room. As he was tugging on him, Chief Collig said, "Hands off me, kid." Frank was so surprised he dropped him and stepped back. In one motion Collig rolled over and stood up, holding his chest with one hand. He glanced down and checked his palm. There was no blood.

Before Frank could react, the chief whipped out his gun, and using the edge of the door for cover, aimed outside and squeezed off three shots.

The Electro-Wizard van sped out of the parking lot and onto the expressway ramp.

"Are you all right?" Frank asked the chief.

"I guess so," he replied. "Thanks to this vest." Frank could tell that the man was shaken.

Joe ran to join them from the motel lobby. "They're getting away!" he shouted.

"Get back inside!" Collig roared. He quickly radioed headquarters for assistance, then jumped into his cruiser and sped off, saying, "I'm sending backup to pick up the Capacs," as he left.

Joe and Frank watched the cruiser speed up the expressway ramp, hearing the siren's wail recede as the vehicle rocketed into the fast-moving traffic.

The brothers turned to look at each other. Frank's heart was still beating wildly. He could see that Joe was as keyed up as he was. "Our friend Carlos is pretty hot property right now," he said.

"Everybody seems to want a piece of him," Joe agreed.

"I guess the police are going to come soon to take him and his mom to New York."

"Are you thinking what I'm thinking?" Joe asked. "If they take Carlos and his mom into custody at their consulate—"

"Then no one in the United States will be able to help them," Frank concluded. "A foreign embassy or consulate is immune from U.S. law."

"You mean if Micola's people get hold of them, our police or government can't do anything to help them?" Joe said.

Frank nodded. The Hardys looked at each other. Then, without a word, they returned to the doorway of the motel where Carlos and his mother were waiting.

"Señora Capac, Carlos," Frank said gallantly, "May we offer you a ride?"

Carlos explained to his mother, who agreed to leave with the Hardys. As they pulled out of the parking lot, they heard the sound of sirens moving closer.

"Where to?" Frank asked.

"Let's call Dad," Joe suggested. "We're going to need a little help on this case."

Frank picked up the cellular phone installed at the base of the driver's seat and dialed his home number. Fenton Hardy answered. "Hi, Frank," he said. "How was soccer practice?"

"It was okay, Dad," Frank answered. "Joe and I made a new friend. He's from Payumac."

"Good. Why don't you bring him over for dinner?"

"I was hoping you'd say that," Frank said. "Can we bring his mother, too? They're in a bit of trouble, and we'd like to help them out."

"What kind of trouble?" Fenton asked.

"I'll explain later," Frank said. "Let's just say

we could all use a place to relax. It's been a long day."

"Let me ask your mother," Fenton said. In a moment he returned to the line. "There's plenty of food," he said. "And it's just about ready."

"Great," Frank said. "See you in a bit."

By the time they pulled into the driveway and entered the house, Laura Hardy had set two extra places at the dining room table.

"We're not formal around here," she said, emerging from the kitchen in a cotton sweater and jeans. "Just sit anywhere."

Carlos introduced his mother, and then spoke rapidly in Spanish. Señora Capac nodded graciously.

"Bienvenidos a mi casa," Laura Hardy said.

Señora Capac's smile showed that she was happy to hear her own language. *"Gracias,"* she said.

"Hey, Mom," Joe said. "I didn't know you could speak Spanish."

Laura smiled and said, "It's pretty rusty, but I remember some of what I learned in school."

Señora Capac offered to help Laura in the kitchen while Fenton sat down at the table with his sons and Carlos. Gazing at the three for a moment, he said, "I got a call from the police about ten minutes ago." The three young men were silent. "Do you guys want to tell me anything?"

"I can explain, Dad," Frank said. "You see—"

Fenton raised his hand to interrupt Frank. "Chief Collig explained enough. I know you disobeyed his order."

"But, Dad," Frank said. "They were going to take Carlos and his mom to the Payumac consulate."

"Which isn't safe for them," Joe added. He explained the note and the danger at the consulate.

"I see," said Mr. Hardy. "I didn't realize it was so serious." He stood up from the table.

Just then Laura Hardy emerged from the kitchen, wearing two oven mitts and carrying a casserole. Fenton smiled apologetically. "You all go ahead," he said. "I've got to make a call."

"Oh, Fenton," Laura said. "Must you? Right this minute?"

"Afraid so," he replied. "But I'll only be a second."

In fact, the call took about twenty minutes. By the time Fenton returned to the table, the others had finished their meal. "Good news," he said, sitting down. "I got an FBI agent to come here tomorrow to question Señora Capac so she and Carlos won't have to go to New York. For now, Carlos and his mother can stay here. Your aunt Gertrude is out of town for a few days, so her room is free. I also asked the FBI to talk to Collig so everything will be squared with him."

Carlos translated for his mother, and she said,

47

"Gracias." Covering the Ixilan woman's hand with her own, Laura Hardy smiled sympathetically.

Fenton turned to his sons and said, "Why don't you get started on the dishes? I want to talk to Carlos privately."

Frank and Joe cleared the table while Fenton and Carlos went into the study. Señora Capac and Laura Hardy moved into the living room. Laura's Spanish had improved during the meal, and now she was speaking more freely with her guest. Judging from the way Señora Capac was speaking quietly with tears in her eyes, Frank guessed they were talking about her kidnapped husband.

While they loaded the dishwasher, Joe and Frank speculated about what to do next. They reviewed the events of the day. "The evidence all points toward Micola," Frank said. "He's named in the kidnapping note, and because of the electrician's wolf's head ring we can link him to the murder attempt back in the locker room."

Looking out the kitchen window, Joe shivered. "Do you think Chief Collig caught the guys who shot at him?"

"I doubt it," Frank replied. "We would have heard. I just hope they can't trace Carlos and his mom here."

"I wonder what Dad and Carlos are talking

about," Joe said. "They've been at it a long time."

Just then they heard the door to the study open and Fenton's voice drifted out. "Frank? Joe? Can you come here for a moment?"

Carlos was settled comfortably in one of the leather wing chairs in Fenton's study. Frank and Joe sat on the couch facing him, and Fenton leaned against the edge of his desk.

"We've been talking about the situation down in Payumac," Fenton said. "And I made a couple of telephone calls to friends at Immigration. It seems that Carlos's father could be in deep trouble."

"Has anyone spotted him?"

"Not exactly," Fenton said. "But there was a flight that left JFK airport about two hours ago with a destination of Telos, Payumac. It was a diplomatic flight, so the passenger list is classified, but it was a nonscheduled flight."

"My father is on that plane," Carlos stated flatly. "I know it."

Fenton explained, "Micola is dangerous, according to my FBI source. Apparently he has done this before, killing or kidnapping his opponents."

"Wow," Joe said.

"And the folks down at the FBI suspect that Micola has rigged the election in Payumac, using terrorist tactics to intimidate Mr. Capac," Fenton said.

"Real democratic," Frank commented sarcastically.

"But now that the FBI knows about Carlos's dad," Joe said, "they'll intervene, won't they?"

"Unfortunately they can't," Fenton said. "The U.S. can't go into another country and force the government to hold fair elections. We have no jurisdiction in a foreign country."

Carlos, Frank, and Joe stared glumly at one another. Joe said, "So we can't do anything, is that what you're saying?"

"*I* think something can be done," Frank said.

Fenton reacted with exasperation. "I don't think I'm going to like what you're about to say."

"We could go tonight," Frank urged. "They've got a two-hour lead, and for every minute we wait, Carlos's dad gets farther away."

Carlos sat up in his chair, his eyes reflecting his newfound hope. Fenton merely shook his head. "It's too dangerous," he said simply and decisively.

Frank said, "You always say, 'The first rule of good detective work is never to allow the trail to get cold.'"

At that moment they heard a knock on the study door. Laura Hardy and Señora Capac walked in. Laura's expression was distressed, and she came right to the point. "Fenton, dear, you know I don't often interfere with your work, but we've got to do something about the Capacs' situation."

"Like letting us go to Payumac to find Señor Capac?" Joe said.

Laura said, "Fenton, we must. The boys have been to foreign countries on their own before."

Fenton ran a hand over his eyes. "Laura, I just don't think it would be safe. I mean, Payumac is over three thousand miles away, ruled by a dictator, and embroiled in major political upheaval. If anything should happen to them, I couldn't live with myself."

"Obviously I agree that we can't let anything happen to the boys," Laura said, "but we must try to help. I can't imagine the Payumac government would consider two teenage boys to be a threat."

Fenton said, "I suppose they could go now, and I could join them soon."

"Cool," Joe said.

"Hold on, Joe," Fenton said. "We have to take this one step at a time." He paused, thinking for a moment. "You boys should be safe because there will be lots of foreigners in the city for the world soccer championship. Wear soccer jackets so everyone thinks you're just fans."

"Of course," Frank and Joe chimed.

* * *

Later that night Frank woke up under the gentle prodding of his father. He checked his clock; it was 5:30 A.M. "Rise and shine," Fenton said. "I'll drive you to the airport."

The words themselves were enough to make Frank alert. He woke his brother, then Carlos. Together, they dressed, with Frank and Joe putting on soccer jackets.

At the airport the boys said a hasty goodbye to their father because they were late. After showing their passports, they picked up their tickets at the check-in counter. "Will you be checking any bags?" asked the attendant.

"No," Frank said. "We just have carry-on luggage. And this." He held up his soccer ball.

With their tickets in hand, the three boys raced down the concourse to their gate. The waiting area was already empty. Frank and Carlos disappeared down the jetway. Joe was the last to board because he lingered for a moment with the pretty flight attendant who took his ticket. "Will you be on the plane?" he asked.

She smiled at him and nodded. Looking over his shoulder, she said, "Oh, it looks like there's one last passenger."

Joe turned and saw a familiar profile.

"I guess this isn't his flight after all," the pretty attendent said after she'd waited for him. "Well, you'll have to find your seat now. We're ready for takeoff." She began to close the door to the jetway.

With a jolt, Joe realized the man he had been looking at was none other than the Gray Man.

"Wait a minute," Joe said, holding the door open. "What is *he* doing here?"

Chapter

7

JOE RACED down the aisle of the plane and found Frank and Carlos buckled into their seats. "Come quick to the jetway!" he said. "I just saw the Gray Man!"

"What?" Frank said in disbelief.

"You mean an old man?" Carlos asked.

Frank chuckled. "He's not literally gray. His name is Mr. Gray. He's sort of a friend of ours who works for a secret U.S. government agency." Speaking to Joe, he asked, "Did he see you?"

Joe shook his head. "I don't think so, but who knows." Before they could decide what to do, they heard the announcement that the plane was starting to taxi. Since they were in the rear of the jumbo jet, they could see the backs of almost all the seats ahead of them. The flight was full of tourists, most of them going to the soccer championships.

"The Gray Man must be following us," Joe said. "It can't be a coincidence that he was here at this hour."

Frank said, "I don't think it's *us* he's following," indicating Carlos. Carlos returned his gaze, obviously confused. "Me?" he asked. "Why would this secret U.S. agency follow me?"

"Because of who you are. The son of the opposition leader in Payumac. They monitor international politics all the time."

"Remember when we showed you the picture of that man wearing the wolf's head ring?" Joe said, changing the subject. "You said it was a symbol for the military police, *los lobos blancos*. Could you tell us more about this group?"

"Yes," Carlos said. "Only new recruits wear the rings. They signify that the recruits have not yet killed for Micola's cause. After a recruit has killed, he wears a badge on his shirt."

"Gruesome," Joe said. "So our electrician friend is a recruit."

Frank said, "And he was trying to earn his badge by knocking off Carlos."

Again they were interrupted, this time as the four jet engines roared into maximum thrust, and the giant airplane rocketed down the runway.

As the plane leveled out at thirty-five thousand

feet, several passengers unbuckled their seat belts and stood up to stretch their legs.

"Or maybe he was trying to give Carlos a warning," Joe said, answering Frank's earlier comment.

"Warn me about what?" Carlos said. "They already kidnapped my father."

"Maybe they didn't plan to kill you, only to say, 'Don't mess with us,'" Frank said.

Joe said, "Well, we're going to mess with them. Big time. So, what's our first move when we land?"

"My mother said to visit my aunt, Marta Capac," Carlos replied. "She teaches at the Peace Institute. She knows a lot of important people. Maybe she's heard where they took my father—if he is still alive," he added.

"We have to hope he's all right," Frank said simply. "Now, it's a seven-hour flight." He slouched down in his seat. "I'm going to get some shut-eye, and I suggest you try to sleep also."

An hour before they were to land, Joe woke from a nightmare involving Carlos. He was in a panic, until he observed that Carlos was safe in the seat next to him, a blanket thrown over his lap.

Shaking the horrible images from his mind, he blinked and peered at Frank. He, too, was asleep. Joe turned to look out the window. Below him was the South American continent, carpeted with the greenery of the rain forest, stretching from horizon to horizon. Joe wondered what mysteries lurked down there.

Do we really know what we're getting into? Joe wondered.

His brother and Carlos were awakened a little while later by the announcement that the pilot had begun his descent into Payumac.

Joe could now make out the volcano Carlos had mentioned, El Gigante, "the Giant." Its rugged cone-shaped height rose naked and black above the surrounding humps and crevasses of forested foothills. Ahead, Joe caught a glimpse of the Pacific Ocean.

"How far is the volcano from Telos?" he asked.

"It is about four hundred kilometers inland," Carlos said. "The capital itself is located on the coast."

"Looks closer than that," Frank said.

"In a straight line, it is closer," Carlos said. "But there are no straight lines in Payumac. The roads have to twist to climb over the mountains and down into the valleys."

As the plane descended, the three grew silent. The city was at sea level, nestled in a valley of the Andean mountain range. Beaches lined the coast like white ribbon dividing the ocean from the land.

As the plane came in low for its final approach, they saw the brand-new soccer stadium, brightly lit in the gathering twilight.

"The championships will last another week or so," Carlos said.

"We should try to take in a game," Joe suggested.

Frank just stared at him, not believing what Joe had said. "Take in a game?" he finally managed. "You're crazy."

The huge jumbo jet finally settled onto the bumpy runway. As they waited for the seat belt sign to go off, Joe leaned into the aisle and peered forward. He could see all the way up to the front of the plane.

A man was standing near the front of the plane, pulling down his bag from an overhead bin. Joe noticed him because the seat belt sign was still lit, and nobody else in the plane was standing. Then Joe saw the guy's profile. His stomach lurched when the man's eyes locked on his.

"Hey!" Joe shouted. "It's him! It's that guy from the electrician's truck!" He flipped open his seat belt buckle and bolted down the aisle. Unfortunately, the seat belt sign went off, and all three hundred passengers stood up, every one anxious to get off the plane. The aisle was instantly clogged. Joe could only move forward a few feet before being stopped by an enormous man who had planted himself squarely in the way.

"I can't move," Joe said, looking back at Frank and Carlos. "He's gone!"

The wait for the line to move was agonizingly slow. By the time Joe finally freed himself from the close quarters of the plane and ran down the jetway, he couldn't find the electrician.

Frank and Carlos joined him a few minutes later, holding their carry-on bags and soccer gear. "I can't believe it," Frank said. "He was on the plane the whole time."

"Can we find out his name?" Carlos said. "Maybe we can look at the passenger list?"

"Not without official clearance," Frank said.

"Speaking of official clearance," Carlos said, "I may have a bit of explaining to do." He nodded in the direction of the customs desks—a row of tables where travelers got their passports stamped and their carry-on bags searched.

"What's the problem?" Joe asked. "This is your country. You have a passport, don't you?"

"Yes," Carlos said, "but what if they recognize my name?"

"So what?" Joe said. "You're a citizen."

"Yes," replied Carlos. "But with Micola in charge, even the customs clerks are working for him."

"We don't have any choice," Frank observed.

"And the longer we wait, the more suspicious they'll get."

The last of the passengers passed through the checkpoint. Just one customs official remained open. Frank stepped up to his desk. His heart leapt to his throat when he saw the wolf's head ring on the man's finger. *Los lobos,* he thought to himself.

Joe was next in line, in front of Carlos. Frank caught Joe's eye and directed his brother's gaze to the ring. Joe nodded, then over his shoulder he whispered, "Get ready to make a run for it."

Carlos tensed but didn't reply.

Frank got checked through without incident, and Joe followed without a hitch. When the customs officer looked at Carlos's passport and saw his name, he hesitated.

A quick sign from Frank, and the three young men sprinted across the line, between the desks, and hightailed it out past the baggage claim area. Carlos led the way onto an escalator. Glancing behind him, Joe saw that several other customs officers were sprinting after them, about fifty yards back. Joe took the escalator two steps at a time. At the top he saw Carlos and Frank dart onto the conveyor belt and duck under the rubber flap that led into the luggage handling area. A couple of passengers gasped in surprise as Joe, too, jumped onto the conveyor belt and rode under the flap, right behind a large square suitcase.

"Where are you guys?" he called out. He saw no sign of his brother or Carlos in the cramped, dark room full of stacked luggage.

"Shhh!" Frank's head popped up from behind a steamer trunk. "Get down!"

"Bad idea, folks," Joe said. "Too many people saw us duck in here." He peeked back into the passenger waiting area, where about twenty people were still waiting for their luggage. The customs officials were fanning out among the crowds. One of the officers started questioning a couple of people. With a sinking feeling, Joe saw the passengers point in their direction. The officer drew his gun and began to advance toward the conveyor belt with a grim look on his face.

Chapter

8

"Move it," Joe shouted. "A guy's on his way in, and he's got a gun."

Spying a chute marked *Equipajes* at the back of the baggage handling room, Joe nimbly climbed over the jumble of suitcases, Frank and Carlos following. Entering the chute feet-first, Joe slid down the steep metal slide, tumbling at the bottom onto a large pile of suitcases, duffel bags, and cardboard boxes. A second later Carlos joined him, then Frank. They were at the ground level of the airport's baggage handling area. The air smelled of diesel fuel and jet exhaust, and they could hear the roar of airplane traffic outside.

"Quick," Joe said, grabbing a steamer trunk.

"Help me shove this up the chute." In a moment, the three had created a barrier against their pursuers.

"That won't hold them very long," Frank said. "This place will be swarming with uniforms any minute."

"This way," Carlos said. He skirted the edge of the luggage pile and led them toward the sunshine that flooded the area outside the luggage garage.

They emerged under the nose of a jumbo jet. Carlos waved them toward the corner of the airport terminal, where they found a grassy hill leading up to the airport's passenger access road. Cars, buses, and taxi cabs rumbled slowly past.

Now that they had left the airfield with its thick exhaust fumes, Frank noticed the distinctive smell of Payumac—jasmine and palm oil wafting on the moist, warm early evening air.

Carlos dashed up the hill and secured a battered taxi. Frank and Joe hung back until they saw his signal. Then all three piled into the rear seat of the sedan. Carlos rattled off their destination, ending with the words *"¡Pronto! ¡Pronto!"* The driver stepped on the accelerator, and the vehicle shot into traffic.

Joe turned around to see if they were being followed. He saw no sign of customs officials— just crowds of tourists. Looking ahead, he surveyed the passing scenery. Palm trees lined the boulevard, with elaborate landscaping all around. "Where are we going?" he asked.

"My *tía*—my aunt—has an apartment in the center of the city," Carlos said. "It is not far from my school. We can drop off our luggage there."

After the taxi passed the soccer stadium and new hotels where all the tourists were staying, the highway narrowed into a two-lane road, with a few streetlights and industrial buildings scattered along the road edge. As they entered the city itself, the buildings became shabbier, closer together, little more than shacks raised off the ground by poles. The palm trees were replaced by weeds and thorny bushes. There was little traffic.

"Not exactly paradise," Frank said.

"No," Carlos said. "Twenty years ago, my father tells me, Telos was a wealthy city, with all the people living in harmony. But after Micola came to power, he took over the factories and transportation companies, firing good workers and replacing them with those loyal to him. Up in the mountains live the victims of his policies— the poorest people of all. Many of them are Ixilans. You see the fires?" He pointed out the window at the nearby mountainside, where tiny glimmers of light glowed. "These people often go for days without eating, or by scavenging at the city dumps. They cook over fires of burning trash. It is a miserable life."

He paused for a few moments, and both the Hardys knew instinctively not to speak. Soon Carlos went on. "It is Micola's fault. He is a corrupt man."

Joe glanced out the window again, watching the streets pass by. No children played in the barren yards. It was so different from his neighborhood back home.

In the city itself, the commercial buildings were in poor repair. Many of the storefronts were covered with iron gates or plywood, and trash clogged the gutters.

They clambered out of the battered taxi in front of an old apartment building. Frank noted that it must have been elegant in some bygone era. Built around a central cobblestone courtyard, the building featured balconies on each floor. There were no lights on any of the landings, making it seem to Frank as if the whole place were deserted.

Carlos led them up a staircase to the third terrace, where potted plants and a garden table stood outside.

Nobody responded to his knock. "Maybe she's out," Joe suggested. "Is she married?"

Carlos shook his head. "She could be working late," he said. "But she is usually home by this time."

"Do you have a key?" Frank asked.

"No," Carlos said, "but I think she keeps a

spare key under one of her plants." He went over to check under a fern. "Yes, here it is."

The apartment, lit by moonlight, was lavishly furnished with antique furniture and thick carpets. Carlos flicked a switch, but no lights came on. "Must be a blackout," he told the Hardys.

They wandered through the silent rooms. The hallway was pitch-dark. As they passed through it, Joe kicked something small and metal, sending it clattering across the marble floor. He picked it up and held it close to his eyes. "A bracelet," he said, adding, "it has the same pattern as your tattoo."

"Yes, the Ixilan motif," Carlos said, examining it. "Why would it be in the hallway?"

Frank said from the room just ahead of them, "Maybe the answer's in here."

It was Marta Capac's bedroom, and in it clothes were piled on the bed in a heap with several pairs of shoes scattered across the floor. The closet doors stood open, and inside was only yawning, empty blackness. "Looks like she's gone," Frank said, glancing in.

Holding the bracelet, Joe added, "And she must have left in a hurry."

Carlos stood in the doorway and said, "There was trouble here. This is not normal."

"Can you call any of her friends?" Frank asked. "Maybe one of the neighbors?"

"Perhaps somebody at school would know where she is," Carlos said.

Joe picked up the phone by the bed. "Can't call. This thing's dead."

"Let us try the dormitories at my school," Carlos said. "My friends are there; perhaps they have heard something. Tía Marta is a favorite teacher."

"Okay," Frank said. "It's a start. But I think we should split up. I want to call Mom and Dad and let them know we arrived safely."

"You will have to go to the international phone center," Carlos said. "It is not too far from here. That is the only way to call out of the country."

Carlos gave Frank detailed instructions about how to find the phone center, and then how to find the dormitories at the Instituto de la Paz.

Leaving the apartment, they moved through the silence of the dark courtyard again. All the darkened doorways gave Joe the creeps. He whispered to Carlos, "It's as though somebody is watching us, but it's too dark to see."

"Yes," Carlos said. "In Telos you must watch all around you. The unexpected can happen."

Frank said goodbye to his brother and Carlos at the street corner and headed for the phone center located on Las Ramblas, Telos's outdoor shopping mall. It was a street without cars, full of pushcart vendors, open storefronts, park benches.

Many Telos citizens were out for an evening stroll. Frank joined the crowds, blending in with the other tourists in his soccer jacket.

He worked his way toward the phone center. He saw no military uniforms—no uniforms at all, in fact.

Fenton Hardy answered on the first ring. "That you, Frank?" came his voice across the static-charged wires. "Is everything all right?"

"Sure, Dad," Frank said. "But we didn't find Carlos's aunt, Marta Capac, at home. It looks like somebody got to her or she cleared out. Have you found out anything there?"

"As a matter of fact, I have," Fenton said. "But I don't know what to make of it. Ask Carlos if he knows an Umberto Corazón."

"I'll ask."

"This Umberto is involved in the anti-Micola underground resistance. They call themselves the *Gente para liberación*—or 'People for Freedom.' They're radical and dedicated to overthrowing Micola."

Frank said, "Sounds like they might be supporters of Carlos's dad."

"I doubt it," Fenton said. "Capac is a pacifist, and this group is violent. In fact, Umberto is promoting violence and revolution. He's armed, but it's not clear how many people are supporting him."

"What does he have to do with finding Carlos's dad?" Frank said.

"I'm not sure if there is a connection, but one

thing is for sure," Fenton said, "Payumac is heating up. Frankly, I'm worried."

"What specifically do you mean, Dad?"

"Well, Payumac has suddenly become the biggest importer of methane gas in all of South America. A huge shipment arrived there by ship about two weeks ago."

"Two weeks," Frank said. "Right around the time Micola planted the bomb in Señor Capac's car. What is methane gas used for?"

"Industrial applications, mostly," Fenton said. "It's a totally legitimate shipment. By itself, methane gas isn't illegal. But the shipment far exceeds the country's annual consumption, and there have been rumors for the last year or so that Payumac is building up its offensive military weapons."

"Can you use the gas in weapons?" Frank asked.

"Have you ever heard of a scram-jet cannon?" his father asked.

"No."

Fenton's voice took on a serious tone. "It's brand-new technology, very powerful, very top secret. It uses methane gas to propel smart bombs to their targets. It's a cross between a cannon and a launching pad. The range of this weapon is enormous because the missiles fly so fast. They reached supersonic speeds in experiments."

Frank let out his breath. "And you say the gas shipment is here already?"

"That's the odd thing," Fenton continued. "The destination for the methane gas was Soledad. That's Carlos's hometown, isn't it?"

"Right," Frank said. "It sounds like I'd better ask Carlos what he thinks of all this."

"Yes," Fenton said. "But I want a report back, Frank. I'm very concerned and want you and Joe out of there if it gets too volatile."

After he hung up, Frank paused for a second. His father wasn't usually so worried, so this must be beyond the range of their usual cases.

Still at the telephone, with his back toward the door, Frank felt the hairs on the back of his neck tingle. It was too quiet.

He whirled around and watched as two *lobos blancos* stepped inside. They said nothing, but they had their guns drawn.

Frank didn't pause to think—he bolted for the opposite door. He almost made it through, but a third guard appeared in the doorway and blocked his exit. Frank didn't stop. He dropped his shoulder, ready to hit the guard at midsection and plow right over him.

He never made contact. Or if he did, he didn't know it, because the guard brought the butt of his gun down on the back of Frank's head, knocking him unconscious.

Chapter

9

UNAWARE OF FRANK'S CAPTURE by *los lobos,* Joe and Carlos made their way toward the Instituto de la Paz. There were almost no lights in this part of town. Shadows in doorways were inky black, and under the occasional streetlight, which cast a bluish glow, the buildings and cars in the street appeared cold and forbidding. Joe and Carlos passed a few people on the streets, mostly men, but it was too dark to make out faces.

Joe could tell Carlos was on the lookout—he kept turning his head and listening.

"Do you feel it?" Carlos asked finally.

"What?" Joe asked.

"They are following us."

"Who?"

"Los lobos," he said.

"Do you see them?" Joe asked.

Carlos shook his head. "But I can tell. Here you will always find Micola's men. Or they find you."

A car came down the street behind them, its headlights cutting a bright path. Caught in its beams ahead of them was a man in a cowboy hat and poncho sitting on a chair in the middle of the sidewalk. He was picking at the guitar he was holding, not really playing. Joe saw him squint against the light.

Without warning a man about Joe's height stepped out from the shadows and gripped his arm. In a husky voice he said, "Your jacket, it is for sale?" His breath smelled sour.

Joe stepped clear of him. "Hands off, man," he said gruffly as he saw someone shove Carlos into an alleyway and disappear into the darkness. "Carlos!" Joe called out, but the stinking man was right in his face.

"No, no, I must have the jacket for the soccer games. International friends, eh?"

Joe tried to step around him in order to follow Carlos, but the stranger kept blocking him.

"I said, back off!" Joe shouted, shoving the man backward. Caught off guard, the man tripped and rolled, howling with pain. Joe dashed into the alley after Carlos.

At first Joe couldn't see a thing. He slowed his

run to a trot while his eyes adjusted to the dark. The alley was strewn with trash, and the sickening smell of rotting garbage smothered his mouth and nose. He arrived at a second alley leading off into darkness. He stopped to listen.

He heard two voices up ahead, but before he could investigate a body slammed into his back, knocking him down on his face. He tried to twist away, but the man was too quick and hopped on him, bending his arm nearly to the breaking point.

"Umberto!" shouted Joe's assailant. "¡Aquí!"

Joe heard two sets of footsteps approach. With his face pressed to the ground, he couldn't see a thing. He heard Carlos's voice, strained and fearful. "Let him go! He's done nothing."

The man sitting on Joe's back pulled him up to a standing position, keeping a firm grip on Joe's twisted arm.

Joe was stunned when he saw that Carlos's assailant was the electrician from Bayport. His black eyes glittered in the moonlight, and his mustache partly covered his sneer.

Umberto held a knife to Carlos's throat. "Welcome to Payumac, my American friend," he said. "Are you enjoying your visit so far?"

"Thanks," Joe answered sarcastically. "You make a guy feel right at home."

"Shut up," growled Joe's captor, shoving his arm higher and making Joe wince with pain.

"Umberto, say what you have to say, then we will leave," he finished to his friend.

Umberto said, "I was just telling Carlos here that he should join me, but he has refused." He glanced down at Carlos, turning the knife so the moonlight flashed along the blade. "His father will be dead in a couple of days, which serves my purposes very well. But his son could be very useful to me alive."

"What are you talking about?" Joe asked.

"When the news gets out about el señor Capac's death, I plan to launch a little revolution. It would help if Carlos could convince the Ixilans to join me in my uprising against Micola."

Joe was thinking fast. "So you're not with *los lobos?*"

Umberto laughed. "It was easy to infiltrate *los lobos.* Our assignment was to eliminate Carlos and to kidnap his father." He tightened his grip around Carlos's throat.

Hoping to distract Umberto from hurting Carlos, Joe said, "When is this revolution going to take place?"

"Two or three days," Umberto said, his voice betraying his pride. "After twenty years of oppression, we shall break the back of Micola's power."

"Where is my father?" Carlos burst out.

Umberto glanced at the captive boy. "Forget him, *niño.* His pacifist ways will never work. Join me, help me and my revolution. It is the only way."

He was interrupted by the sound of screeching tires at the far end of the alley. The man holding Joe shoved him into a pile of cardboard boxes, which collapsed over him. By the time he freed himself, a police car with flashing red lights had skidded to a stop, blocking the entrance to the alley. Two men leapt out from the car and tackled him. A pair of cold handcuffs were snapped to his wrists behind his back.

As the police pulled him to his feet and dragged him to their waiting car, he saw that Carlos, too, had been captured. Before climbing into the police car, he looked around for Umberto. There was no sign of him—just a man in a poncho on a chair, holding a guitar and speaking into a walkie-talkie.

Frank woke with a pain at the back of his head. He touched the bruise with his fingers and felt the tender lump. Looking around, he saw he was in a jail cell with his brother and Carlos. Early morning light filtered through barred windows high above him.

Joe and Carlos were still asleep on the thin pads that served as mattresses. The walls were the drab gray of cement block, with a rusted iron door providing the only entrance—and only escape.

Frank shook Joe's shoulder gently. His brother awoke, squinting against the light and rubbing his eyes. "Do you know where we are?" Frank asked.

"Micola's headquarters," Joe said sleepily. "We tried to wake you last night when they brought us in, but you were out cold."

"My head hurts," Frank said.

"You have a nasty cut," Joe said. "I cleaned it up as best I could."

"They got me at the phone center," Frank explained, "after I talked to Dad."

"We never got to Carlos's school," Joe admitted. "But we did run into our old friend, the electrician." He briefly explained Umberto's planned revolution and his infiltration of *los lobos*.

"Umberto Corazón?" Frank said incredulously. "Dad was telling me about him."

"What is happening?" Carlos said groggily from his mattress.

"A little coincidence," Joe said. But before he could explain, all three boys heard the keys jangle in the door. The hinges screamed as the rusty metal door swung open, revealing a woman of about thirty-five, tall and slender, with a great mass of black hair curling around the shoulders of her prisoner's coverall. She was beautiful, with intelligent clear brown eyes and an oval face.

Two guards entered the room with her and

closed the door behind them. Carlos rushed to embrace her. *"Tía,"* he cried.

"Carlos," she said, lifting her hands to hug him. Frank saw that she was wearing handcuffs, but she managed to clasp her nephew close in spite of them. "You're alive! I'm so grateful."

"So you're Marta Capac," Joe said. "We've been trying to find you." She greeted him with a smile that made Joe's heart beat a little faster.

"What happened to you?" Carlos asked her.

"I was arrested yesterday," she answered in English. Eyeing the guards, she added, "And they weren't very nice about it."

"Did they hurt you?" Carlos asked, his anger rising. "Because if they did—"

"No," Marta Capac said. "Nothing like that."

Frank could contain his curiosity no longer. "Do you have news of Señor Capac? We know he's in the country somewhere. And we have reason to believe his life is in danger."

"I heard the guards talking yesterday," she said. "He has been taken to Soledad."

"Isn't that your hometown?" Frank asked.

"Yes," Carlos replied. "It is near the volcano."

"Didn't the kidnapper's note mention something about the 'fire'?" Frank pressed.

"That is right!" Carlos said. "It said he would die in the *fuego del Gigante.*"

"Just as the old legends predicted," Marta

Capac said. She blinked back her tears. "My poor, poor brother. He is so foolish."

"Foolish?" Carlos said. "How can you say that?"

"I mean innocent," Marta Capac said. "He always was. So trusting."

They were interrupted by keys in the door and the squeal of metal against metal. In the doorway stood a short man, about five foot seven or eight, wearing a trim uniform of combat fatigues. Strapped across his chest was a leather harness, studded with ammunition. He wore a gun at his hip and a hat, decorated with a wolf's head insignia on its brim. His eyes glittered like black ice.

"Wait outside," he told the two guards who had accompanied Marta Capac. The two guards snapped to attention, and Frank guessed that this man was Micola himself.

Joe didn't need more than a first impression to decide that this man was evil. It wasn't his physical presence—after all, Joe could have taken him down with a full-body tackle—but it was those shifty, coal black eyes that bored through everything in their path.

Micola's gaze came to rest on Carlos. "Have a little accident, young man?" the military dictator asked, nodding at Carlos's sling. Carlos didn't answer, but Joe knew that under his passive exterior Carlos was smoldering. "Not speaking today?" Micola taunted after a moment of silence. "What's the matter, boy?"

Frank was the one to finally speak. "Listen, you seem to have some kind of problem here, but my brother and I aren't part of it. And right now, you're illegally holding two American citizens. I demand to be allowed to call my embassy."

Micola shifted his eyes to Frank, measuring him in a single glance. "I'm afraid you won't be talking to your fellow countrymen for a while. Your embassy won't help you here, boy," he growled.

"That is illegal," Frank said.

"You want the law?" Micola shouted suddenly. "Well, you're looking at the law, and the law says you are to die."

Joe's throat constricted and his mouth became dry. Something in Micola's voice told him the man was used to killing and wouldn't hesitate to do it again.

Calling in the guards, Micola said, "Take them." He left without looking back.

The guards handcuffed Frank, Joe, and Carlos, then led the four prisoners down the hall to an iron gate. Their handcuffs jingled as they walked, but no one spoke.

They emerged into the early morning sun, squinting. Frank quickly got his bearings. They were in the foothills above the city. He could see all of Telos spread below them.

Parked by the curb was a canvas-covered military personnel carrier. Micola waited beside the cab. The guards forced Joe and the others to climb into the back of the truck. He sat on one of the two benches that ran along the sides of the truck bed.

One guard joined the four prisoners in the back of the truck, while two more climbed into the cab. Micola appeared at the rear of the truck. *"Adiós,"* he said. "You'll be joining your father shortly." Dramatically he lifted his eyes to the sky. "One way or another."

The truck started with a roar. Over the rumbling, Frank shouted, "Where are we going?"

"To the volcano, boy!" returned Micola. "I'll join you the day after tomorrow for the sunrise ceremony."

"What ceremony?" Frank asked.

"The one where we put Tsotal to sleep!" The truck pulled away from the building. It turned uphill, heading west, away from the city of Telos.

Joe was sitting next to Marta Capac. "Why does he keep talking about Tsotal?" he asked.

Marta Capac looked at him with an ironic smile. "Carlos hasn't told you about the legends of the Ixilan people?"

"No," Joe answered. "Except that—"

"*¡Silencio!*" shouted the guard, gesturing with his gun at the pair. Joe flinched as the barrel of the gun touched his face.

Frank was glaring at him, and at first Joe thought he was angry for provoking the guard. But then Frank's eyes dropped down to his lap. Joe followed his gaze and saw one of Frank's hands emerge from his soccer jacket, clutching something in his fist. Frank opened his palm, showing Joe a small metal object about as long as a hairpin.

Joe recognized the needle valve, a thin metal device that, when attached to a pump, helped inflate soccer balls. It was standard equipment for the sport, as common as shin pads. But here, in the truck, Joe knew the needle valve would have another purpose. With Frank's nimble fingers, he could probably pick the locks on their handcuffs.

"Hey, you," Joe said, thinking he'd distract the guard for a while. "I heard the Payumac soccer team is just a bunch of sissies."

"*¡Silencio!*" said the guard again. Then, gesturing at Joe, he said to Carlos, "*¿Qué dijo?*"

Carlos said, "He wants to know what you said."

Joe grinned. "Tell him."

Carlos rattled off the translation, and the guard grew livid. He pointed the gun at Joe's chest. "*¡Idiota!*" he shouted. Moving in a crouch to avoid the low ceiling of the canvas roof, he moved forward, raising the butt of the gun in order to strike him.

Frank was ready, having sprung the lock on his handcuffs. He tripped the guard, at the same time knocking the gun out of his hand. With the guard on the floor, Frank brought down a solid judo chop to his head.

Frank grabbed the man's keys. Joe was already moving, and with his still-cuffed hands he grabbed one of the guard's hands. "Get the other one," he said to Marta Capac.

She was watching their struggle with horror, but at Joe's command she quickly stepped on the wrist of the guard, pressing his arm to the floor.

Together, they held the man down. "Give me your sock," Frank said to Carlos as he unlocked the handcuff from his other wrist. "We've got to gag him." While Frank used his handcuffs to secure the guard to one of the bench legs that was bolted to the floor, Carlos removed his shoe and pulled off his sock, tying the cotton tube around the guard's mouth.

Frank quickly freed Carlos, then Joe, and finally Marta Capac. The four of them clustered at the rear tailgate. "We're going too fast to jump," Joe said in Frank's ear, watching the pavement whizz by under the speeding truck.

Frank pointed to the thick vegetation that lined

the road. "Try to make it onto the shoulder of the road," he said.

Frank helped Marta Capac, then launched himself into the air, with Joe and Carlos immediately behind. Joe closed his eyes when his feet left the truck. He didn't want to see what he was going to hit.

Chapter

10

JOE LANDED AND ROLLED onto the soft dirt along
the highway. He scraped his arm, but was otherwise unhurt. Frank had landed a few feet behind
him, and he joined Joe.

Together they helped Carlos and Marta Capac
up. She said, "I almost didn't jump. If you had
not helped me, I would still be on the truck."
Her hair was hanging around her face as she
dusted off her palms. She was very beautiful, with
her face flushed from the excitement of their escape, and her dark eyes alive with exhilaration.

Carlos tossed his sling into the grass, saying, "I
have no need of this!" Then he led his aunt and
the Hardys into the jungle to find help. By
Frank's calculations, they were about twenty

some miles from Telos, probably at an altitude of about six thousand feet. The jungle was thick in this tropical climate, and once they had left the cleared area along the road, the foliage closed in around them and covered over the sky above them. The smell of humid greenery was almost oppressive.

About fifty yards into the jungle, the underbrush became a tangled growth perpetually shaded by a thick canopy the trees above made. Carlos was the first to spot the smoke from a fire. Pointing it out to Frank, he said, "There are people nearby, maybe the Ixilans." They plunged into the woods in the direction of the fires.

"Is it wise to meet the people who live up here?" Marta Capac asked. "Their hunger makes them a little crazy." Frank noticed that she was fingering a thin gold necklace.

"You might want to pocket that," he suggested. "Or maybe we could trade it for some information."

She scowled and said unpleasantly, "This was a gift. I will die before I give it up." She removed the chain and placed it in her pocket.

Given their situation, Frank thought her attitude strange, but he apologized anyway. "It was just a thought. I'm sorry."

Ahead of them Carlos was explaining to Joe about the people who lived in the mountains. "We call them the desperate ones," he said.

"They live in cardboard shacks—very poor. Micola doesn't care anything about them. Their living conditions are so harsh that many of them have reverted to the old ways, and they can be very superstitious."

Soon they came to a giant fire laid among the trunks of the tall trees. Here the underbrush had been cleared away and several children were playing as some women watched the approach of the strangers warily. The women were dressed in rags and had the hollow-eyed look of people on the edge of starvation.

The dismal surroundings gave Joe the creeps. He was edgy anyway, fearing that the *lobos* guards from the truck would appear at any moment with their guns blazing.

Carlos, however, seemed perfectly at ease as he approached the women and spoke with them. They gestured back to the road and then looked at the sun's position in the sky.

Carlos reported back to the group that in an hour or so a bus would pass by on the same road they had just left. "It is the bus that goes to Soledad," Carlos said. "Perhaps we can wave it down."

"Sounds risky," Frank said.

"It is our only chance," Carlos said. "We cannot go back to Telos. Micola's men are everywhere. And my father is in Soledad. The bus is the only way to get there."

"I think we should get out of here," said Marta Capac, obviously made uncomfortable by the impoverished women and their children.

The party of four trekked back toward the highway, taking a parallel route to their earlier track. As he stepped over the ancient roots of the tall trees, Frank was alert to every sound. A screech from a spider monkey or the cry of a toucan would startle him. By the time the highway came into view, he was glad to see it even though it, too, meant danger.

Tangled vegetation grew in profusion along the roadside, and they took cover there. Frank could see that they had emerged at a spot well above the point where they had jumped from the truck. The mountain was steep here, with the road twisting snakelike through a series of switchbacks below them.

"Looks like they found the place where we jumped," Joe said, crouching beside Frank. They could see the truck parked at the bottom of the slope on the side of the road. One guard was leaning against a fender, aiming a rifle at the leafy foliage that lined the road.

Joe went back to Marta Capac and Carlos, who remained hidden farther back. "We might as well make ourselves comfortable," Carlos said. "That bus isn't due for another half hour."

Joe saw a patch of long-stemmed grasses growing nearby and flattened some of it to create a cushioned seat. "Lády Capac," he said, "your throne awaits you."

"Thank you," she said with a half smile, sitting carefully. "This is the first time anyone has been this nice to me since—" She paused, then her eyes filled with tears. "Well, since I was taken into captivity. You are very kind, Joe."

It gave Joe a thrill to hear her say his name.

About forty minutes later they watched as the bus arrived. Frank was surprised that it was an old yellow school bus, the kind he and Joe had ridden to elementary school. But this bus was battered and ancient, splattered with mud and emitting clouds of blue-tinted exhaust as it labored up the mountain slope.

The guard beside the truck stepped out into the road and flagged the bus down with his rifle. Once it stopped, Frank saw several men climb out and stand with their heads hanging while the guard questioned them. The guard then searched the bus. When the guard waved the bus ahead, Frank signaled Joe and the four got into position to flag down the bus, which was now negotiating the sharp twists in the road below them.

Marta Capac said, "Let me talk to the driver by myself. A woman will certainly get his attention."

Frank was impressed by her bravery. She seemed like Callie Shaw, his girlfriend back in Bayport—willful and impulsive and courageous.

At other times, though, she was more demure and shy, especially when talking to Joe. Above all, she's smart, he told himself as the bus pulled to a halt beside her.

Whatever Marta Capac said to the driver, a young man wearing a World Cup soccer T-shirt, it worked. At her signal Joe and the others followed her onto the bus. The passengers were all poor mountain people, judging from their rough, hand-loomed clothing.

The bus lurched into gear, and Joe heard the bleating of a goat, which was leaning up against his leg. He scratched its bony head while Marta Capac found some empty seats in the rear of the bus. She motioned for the three boys to join her.

The goat stayed tied up at the front of the bus. As they took their seats, Carlos explained that they were on a second-class bus, far cheaper than the luxurious ones that carried tourists into the mountain regions of Payumac. The Ixilans were used to this form of travel. It was cheap, and best of all they could carry anything they wanted. "If it fits through the door of the bus," he said, "you can bring it with you."

"Like goats?"

Carlos nodded. "Chickens, too. You see, in the rural parts of Payumac, it is customary for a traveler to bring a live animal as a gift. Ixilans are generous people."

Frank noticed several campaign posters plastered to the space above the windows—all featured Micola's face and the words ¡*Vota para mí!*

"Doesn't your father have posters?" Frank asked Carlos.

"Micola controls the transportation system," he replied. "He won't allow my father to promote his candidacy. But he used to speak publicly, and the Ixilans know about him through word of mouth."

"You are so idealistic," Marta Capac said, "just like your father."

Hearing a certain amount of skepticism in her voice, Frank said, "But aren't you confident that Señor Capac will be elected president?"

Marta Capac thought for a moment, then carefully chose her words. "You seem to forget that my brother is a sworn pacifist—he will never fight back. It is a noble position, but the people are used to years of Micola's strong-handed government. Do you think they will vote for someone they think is weak? I call that idealistic."

"There's a way to find out," Joe said. "We could take a poll of the people on this bus. Most of them are Ixilans, right?"

Carlos agreed to ask several passengers about the upcoming elections. "You will see, *tía mía*," he said. "The Ixilans will support my father."

Frank watched Carlos as he stood in the aisle, speaking with passengers near the front, swaying with the movement of the bus as it wound up along the mountain road.

While Carlos was occupied, Joe turned toward Marta Capac. She was more beautiful than ever. "How long does this trip take?" he asked.

"Eighteen hours," she replied.

Joe glanced at his watch. "That puts us in Soledad at six A.M. I hope we get to stop for food sometime before that. Are you hungry?"

"Actually I am," she admitted. "I wonder if the people on this bus are as generous as Carlos claims."

Frank said, "You don't seem to know as much about the Ixilans as your nephew does."

"I do," Marta Capac said a little defensively. "I just haven't been around the rural poor as much as he has." She stood up and asked an old woman sitting ahead of them for food. The old woman smiled warmly and gave them what she had—some bread, goat cheese, water, and dried meat.

As they were eating, Carlos returned to the back of the bus, his eyes blazing. "There's been an earthquake in Soledad," he said. "I couldn't find out how much damage there was, but they told me it was the biggest in memory. The people are saying it's a sign."

"A sign of what?" Frank asked.

"Tsotal," Carlos replied.

Frank let out a low whistle.

"There is more," Carlos said. "According to the legend, the only way to put Tsotal back to sleep is to sacrifice the king of the Ixilans. This will serve Micola's purpose well."

Frank said, "Because your father is a descendant of the ancient kings?"

"Yes. He must be the human sacrifice that stops Tsotal from shaking the earth," Carlos concluded.

Chapter

11

WHEN JOE AWOKE, his neck was stiff. The bus had just pulled to a stop, and the driver had shut off the engine. Joe checked his watch. It was 5:30 A.M.

Frank, too, had just woken up and glanced around. He looked out the window and saw a whitewashed stucco wall about four feet away, glowing dimly in the predawn light. There was something strange about the top of this wall—it was jagged and broken.

When he went out, Frank realized it wasn't a wall at all—it was a house or part of one. The rest of it had collapsed in on itself to become a pile of rubble. Huge sections of wooden floors, slabs of walls, and broken furniture lay in a twisted pile of rubble.

Joe woke up Carlos and Marta Capac, and the three joined Frank outside. As the morning light grew stronger, they could make out more houses in similar states of ruin. Huge cracks crisscrossed the street, and Frank could smell the stench of burnt rubber.

Carlos let out a sigh of despair. "I can't believe it," he said. They were all shocked by the scale of the devastation they saw around them.

The bus driver was saying something in Spanish. Carlos translated for them. "He's saying that he can't drive the bus any farther into town. We'll have to walk from here."

"I wonder how we can find out about the sacrifice," Joe said. "It's not public, is it?"

"I do not know," Carlos said. "There have been no sacrifices for hundreds of years. Maybe I should ask one of the passengers."

Just then he felt a tug on his sleeve. The woman who had shared her food the night before was standing beside Carlos. She was short, less than five feet tall, and wore a wraparound shawl that, on her, was like a blanket.

"Carlos Capac?" she said. "You are the son of el señor Capac?" Her Spanish accent was thick, and her croaking voice nearly made her speech incomprehensible to Carlos, who translated for Frank and Joe.

"Yes," Carlos said, surprised that he didn't know this woman who lived in Soledad. "Who are you? I have been away in Telos for many years."

"Leonora." She eyed the young man, then said, *"Niño,* I show you where your father is. Micola's men brought him to my house for the elders to guard until he can be sacrificed."

Leonora seated them on the now empty bus. "The driver will take me to my home," she explained. Frank was surprised by her motherly treatment of Carlos. She sat beside him and held his hand, her wrinkled face bunched up with worry. *"Tu papá,"* she said. "Very great man. Handsome, like you. And wise. Truly a king!" Her eyes glittered with tears. "So sad he must be sacrificed."

"He won't die," Carlos said. "Not as long as I am alive to help him."

Marta Capac sat behind Carlos, and she leaned forward to put an arm around him. "Carlos," she said sadly.

"Oh, he will be sacrificed," Leonora said. "It is the only way to put Tsotal to sleep. But a son should see his father before he dies—it is only right."

The bus driver climbed back into his seat and shut the doors. *"¿La hacienda de llamas?"* he asked.

"Sí," Leonora said. "It is up on the volcano."

They left Soledad with one last look at the devastation. Then the bus rolled back onto the highway.

With only five passengers, the bus rattled louder than ever as it lumbered out of town, and labored up the steep slope on a gravel road that grew increasingly narrow.

After about ten minutes Carlos said to Leonora, "Tell me where the sacrifice will take place."

"Up on the *tierra de morir*," she said. "The ancient killing grounds at the lip of the volcano. The Ixilan elders will take him up tonight, and tomorrow they will perform the ritual." She gazed out the window at the volcano rising above the jungle greenery, her face reflecting her deep fear of it. "And not too soon. Tsotal is very angry. He will keep shaking the earth until the sacrifice puts him back to sleep."

As if Leonora's words were a prophecy, Joe felt a sudden jolt in the earth beneath the bus. The wheel of the bus turned sharply and was yanked out of the driver's hands. The vehicle fishtailed wildly.

"Watch out!" Joe shouted as the front wheels skidded off the gravel and the entire front end of the bus went over the embankment. A second jolt knocked them sideways, and the undercarriage of the bus scraped loudly on the rocks.

For a second the bus stopped completely, teetering out over empty space with its front end pointing downward. Through the driver's window, Frank could see straight down into a steep, rocky gorge. The view was dizzying—sheer rock walls, with a few scrub trees clinging to outcroppings. At the bottom of the cliff was a river, foaming white where it poured over huge boulders.

Frank held his breath. For a second he thought they wouldn't go over the edge, but another massive vibration in the ground caused the bus to slide and plunge forward, rolling as it slid down the steep embankment.

The bus made a huge racket as it tumbled down the mountainside. Joe's ears were assaulted by the shriek of metal as it tore over naked rocks. The window beside his head exploded, covering him with shards of glass. Joe saw Frank's body fly up to the ceiling, then get tossed forward toward the driver.

When they hit the river, Joe was thrown against the seat in front of him, but he knew he wasn't hurt. Water rushed through the shattered windshield and the front door, which had been ripped from its hinges. The bus began to sink rapidly.

Joe felt Carlos's hands grasp at his waist as the water surged up over them. He fought down a wave of panic, kicked free of the seat, and grabbed Leonora, pulling Carlos along with them. Through a smashed-out window, Joe could see the surface above them, bright and shimmering. Joe could also watch it recede as they sank deeper. He stuck his head through the window, then his shoulders, carefully maneuvering Leonora out ahead of him. Carlos let go of Joe while he slipped out through the narrow space, careful to avoid the sharp edges of broken glass. Holding on to Leonora, he turned to guide Carlos through. Then all three swam up toward the light—and air—as fast as they could.

Meanwhile Frank swam toward the blurry form of Marta Capac. He saw instantly that she was caught between the back of the driver's seat and the first passenger seat. He reached out to grab her elbow as she pointed toward her foot. Frank understood immediately. Her foot was wedged under the driver's seat. He reached down and felt his way down her leg. Before his hand had reached her foot, however, he felt her arm grip his neck from behind.

The pressure around his windpipe forced some of the precious air from his lungs. He grabbed her arm, pulling it away, but she had a firm grip on him. For a second he panicked, but then he forced himself to think rationally. He'd been trained to break the choke hold of a terrified swimmer. Tucking his chin and turning his head, he lifted her arm forcefully upward, while he kicked down with his feet, slipping his face under her arm. It was a tight squeeze, but he managed to free himself.

He was below her now, at the level of her feet. Marta Capac must have freed her own foot because now she was swimming out the empty space where the windshield had been. Frank was surprised at her hasty recovery and her quick escape, but he didn't have time to dwell on it. The bus had settled on the bottom of the river, and his lungs were screaming for air. He swam for the front door. Seeing no one, he assumed everyone was out and shot out the door and rose rapidly to the surface.

When his head broke the surface, Frank took in a huge gulp of air, sweeter than anything he'd ever breathed in his life. He coughed and splashed, aware that the current was swirling around him. Disoriented and choking, he finally made it to a relatively calm pool—a deep section where the current was less powerful. Then he swam to the riverbank.

As Frank pulled himself onto a rock, he saw his brother appear over on the bank. "Are you all right?" Joe shouted over the roaring water.

Between breaths, Frank managed to say, "Yes!"

"Come on up here," Joe returned. "I've got something to show you."

By the time Frank had climbed up the rocky cliff, he was ready to collapse. His wet sneakers felt like heavy weights, and his chest heaved with the effort of climbing. But what he saw made him forget his discomfort.

Marta Capac, Leonora, Carlos, and Joe were looking at something floating in the river at the top of a waterfall. It was the bus driver. He was floating facedown in the water.

At first Frank thought he was still alive, because he was moving slightly, bobbing up and down. "Let's get him," Frank shouted to Joe, "before he drifts over the edge of the waterfall."

"You don't want to go in there again," Joe said. "Look."

Frank saw that several fish were leaping into the air around the body. Leonora turned to look at him through the dripping strands of her long gray hair. "Piranha," she explained in Spanish, as Carlos translated. "Very hungry today." She lowered herself onto a rock, and faced away from the river.

With a sick feeling in his stomach, Frank watched the bus driver's body slip over the falls and out of sight.

Joe shuddered involuntarily. "To think we were all just in that water," he said.

They were all startled by Leonora's croaking voice chanting in Spanish. Frank turned to find her kneeling, with her hands raised. Her eyes were closed. Carlos explained that she was praying for the soul of the dead bus driver as he joined the other immortals in the land of the gods.

Carlos respectfully listened in silence to the old woman's prayers. Joe and Frank bowed their heads out of respect. Only Marta Capac remained aloof, running her fingers through her hair to dry it and gazing up toward the road from which the bus had fallen. Frank inspected her face discreetly. She seemed so harmless now, but whenever he swallowed, Frank was reminded of the tight grip she had had around his throat. Had she been in a drowner's panic? She had seemed so rational, and her grip had been so deliberate.

When Leonora's prayer ended, it took only a moment for Frank to blurt, "How's your foot?" to Marta Capac. Carlos's aunt was distracted, remote. "It's fine," she said. Then she blushed, saying, "I mean, it's a little sore. I must thank you for saving my life."

"You *should* thank me," Frank burst out, "since you nearly took my life when I was saving yours."

"Chill out, Frank," Joe said. He was surprised by his brother's outburst, especially because Frank was usually so calm. "What happened down there?"

"My foot," Marta Capac said. "It was caught under the seat. I was in a panic. When your brother swam over to me, I grabbed onto him."

"Your foot seemed to come free pretty easily," Frank said.

"Wait a minute, both of you," Joe said, uncomfortable with his role as peacemaker. "What are you saying, Frank? That her foot wasn't caught?"

"I don't know what he's talking about," said Marta Capac. "But he's scaring me."

Joe tried to comfort her by putting an arm around her. "We're all upset. Let's just forget it."

Frank saw that pressing his point would only cause an argument, so he decided against it. He did vow to keep a close eye on Marta Capac from then on. With this thought in mind, he extended his hand toward her, saying, "I'm sorry. It was pretty dark down there, and I was running out of air. I must have made a mistake."

Marta Capac took his hand. "As your brother says," she said, "let us forget it. Again, I thank you for saving my life."

Carlos helped Leonora up. *"Gracias,"* she said. "It is not far," Carlos translated.

At the edge of the river, the steep cliff rose nearly vertical to the water, with the road at the top. "Can you climb?" Carlos asked Leonora. Without a word, she began to pull herself up the steep hillside, clinging to vines and toe holds in the rock with the agility of a much younger woman.

As the roaring of the rapids fell behind them, the silence of the mountainside became apparent.

When Joe finally reached the road above, he felt the hot sun drying his T-shirt and jeans. He was breathing hard—the high-altitude air was thin—but he hurried to keep up with Carlos.

The ranch consisted of a small hacienda built in a jungle clearing beside the road. Stone-and-mortar walls supported a grass roof. A battered World War II jeep stood outside a barn. The only visible damage to the building from the earthquake was a collapsed woodshed. Leonora said proudly in Spanish to Carlos, who translated, "Many earthquakes has my home seen, but none has toppled it." She led them into the house through a weathered wooden door. Inside was a child of about ten dressed in just a shift. Probably Leonora's grandchild. The small room was otherwise deserted. Frank saw ashes in the kitchen fireplace smoldering.

Leonora grabbed the child by the shoulders and questioned him. With Carlos translating, the timid child explained that the elders had taken his father to the volcano early that morning.

Leonora shook her head. "They were supposed to wait," she said.

Thinking quickly, Frank said, "Could we borrow that jeep outside?" To Joe and Carlos he said, "Maybe we can catch up to them before they get to the top of the volcano."

"*Sí,*" said Leonora.

"But you won't make it all the way to the top. You'll have to walk, as our people have been doing for thousands of years," Carlos said, translating for Leonora.

Joe was already at the door. "Let's go."

"First, food," Leonora said. "Must eat."

"And water," Frank added. "And we might need some rope."

"In the barn," she said.

The three boys headed out to the barn, while Marta Capac and Leonora stayed to put a meal together. Inside the barn Joe found a coil of cotton rope. Carlos picked up an old horse blanket. Frank saw a pair of saddlebags and asked, "Do they have horses here?"

"No," Carlos answered. He gestured to a stall at the back of the barn, where in the dim light they could make out a llama's head rising above the rough-plank fence of its pen. The large black eyes, white-wool fur, topped by slender ears, made the animal appear rabbitlike, but its long nose and flexible lips made it resemble a camel. Altogether Frank and Joe found him to be rather sweet and comical.

"Can we ride it?" Joe asked skeptically, checking out the short-legged animal whose head was level with his own.

"No," said Carlos. "We use them only as pack animals." The llama had tilted its head curiously, seemingly knowing they were speaking about it.

Before they could load the jeep, Leonora called them into the house to eat. Leaving their equipment by the barn door, they headed inside, where they found a meal laid out by the sturdy old woman. Protesting that they didn't have time, Carlos was soon persuaded by the sight of bread and salted meat.

Before eating, Marta Capac disappeared out the back door. Probably to wash her hands at a pump, Joe thought.

He was ravenous. There was bread and butter, along with a strange kind of cheese, sharp and salty, that Carlos explained was made from llama milk.

"It's not exactly a hamburger and fries," Joe said, "but it's good."

As he was chewing on a piece of salted meat, Frank realized that he didn't know where Marta Capac was. He had vowed to keep her in sight, but before he could do anything about finding her, he heard the sound of a vehicle starting up outside. Rushing to the door, he saw Marta Capac in the jeep, backing away from the barn. She steered the dusty vehicle toward the road leading back to Soledad and peeled away.

Chapter
12

JOE SPRINTED OUT of the ranchhouse behind Frank. The dust raised by the jeep obscured the vehicle itself, but Joe could hear the rattling chassis and the rumble of the engine as it sped off. Frank slowed down to a trot, and Joe caught up to him quickly. The brothers stopped, panting. "She—she just took our—" Frank said.

"I know," Joe said. "That was our ticket up to the volcano. Where is she going?"

"I don't know," Frank said. "But somehow I don't think she's going to help us any."

Carlos joined them. "Where did she go?" he asked.

"We were just trying to figure that out," Frank said.

"Maybe she went down to Soledad to get some help," Joe suggested.

"From whom," Frank said. *"Los lobos?"*

"She wouldn't do that," Carlos said. "It is eighteen hours to Soledad and another eighteen back. My father would be long dead by that time."

"The two of you have to face reality," Frank said. "I know she's your aunt, Carlos, but she's been acting suspiciously." He briefly outlined her underwater death grip. "She wasn't drowning," he concluded. "She knew exactly what she was doing."

"And you think she's gone down to Soledad to make sure we can't rescue her brother?" Joe said. "Come on Frank, you're always telling me not to jump to conclusions. Aren't you doing that now? Carlos's aunt wouldn't betray him and his father."

"Why else would she just take off?" Frank asked. Looking at Carlos, he saw that his friend was in great conflict. "I'm sorry to have to say this, Carlos, but I don't think Marta Capac has your father's best interests at heart."

"No," Carlos said. "It can't be." He turned back toward the house. Frank and Joe followed, concerned.

"Hey, Carlos," Joe said. "At least we still have our climbing gear. And that llama can carry a load."

Carlos paused, looking at his friends. "She didn't even say goodbye," he said sadly. Then he swallowed hard, and his voice took on a hard edge. "Okay, we'll take the llama. We need to hurry now, because the hike is long and difficult."

Frank said, "Now you're talking! Let's go!"

For the second time in an hour, Joe felt the warm juice from the llama's mouth hit the side of his neck. "Ugh," he said again, ducking and wiping the slimy spittle from his skin. "Why does that animal keep spitting at me?"

Carlos laughed. "It is being territorial," he explained. "You have to stay out of its range."

Joe moved toward the side of the trail to allow Carlos to lead the llama. He joined Frank behind the animal.

They were following a trail that wound upward between the trunks of teakwood, gum, and fig trees. For several hours they had trekked through the dense forests, listening to the screeches of spider monkeys high up in the canopy.

With about an hour and a half of sunlight left in the day, the three young men and their llama reached the spine of the ridge, half a mile from where it met the volcano's cone. It took Joe's breath away to see the sweep of land fall sharply away from him on either side. Looking toward his left, Joe saw a deep valley carpeted with the tops of the trees stretching down for a mile or more before leveling out.

On his right was another valley, just as steep and just as densely overgrown. Ahead of him, the volcano's cone rose straight up—a smooth cliff looming high up into the sky, too steep for any vegetation to cling to, its charcoal gray flanks tinted rose with the rays of the setting sun.

"What's that?" Joe asked, pointing to the opposite side of the valley to their right, where yet another ridge rose. The greenery on the far side of the valley was pockmarked with four distinct scars, where naked rock was exposed in the otherwise tree-covered hillside. Above the scars were blackened plumes where a fire had scorched the vegetation.

"I do not know," Carlos said, frowning. "A fire, it looks like."

"Recent, too," Frank said.

"Maybe they're doing some logging," Joe said.

"I doubt it," Carlos said. "There are no roads back there. This is the high country. Most of the logging occurs in the foothills."

Carlos pressed forward, leading the llama along the ridge toward the volcano cone. Joe marveled at how surefooted the animal was. Joe wished for the same confidence. One misstep, one slip, and he would have a long fall.

As they neared the juncture of the ridge and the perpendicular wall of the cone, Carlos began to walk faster, leaving Frank and Joe farther behind. The light was fading as the sun drew closer to the western horizon. Joe began to wonder what it would be like to climb the volcano cone in the dark, when without warning a huge crack of thunder ripped through the air, knocking Joe off his feet.

Frank saw a flash of light below them and to their right, and an object spewing fire rocketed into the air between the two walls of the facing ridges, hurtling at breakneck speed. A second later it slammed into the opposite wall, exploding into a huge fireball that set the surrounding vegetation on fire.

Because of the distance, the sound of the explosion was delayed a second or two, but when it came it was deafening. The llama let loose a high-pitched bray and yanked its harness free from Carlos's hand. Joe thought the animal jumped headfirst down the steep incline behind them, but in a second he saw it fifty feet below, galloping into the trees.

Frank was watching the site of the explosion, and what he saw terrified him. It was as if the entire valley were a carpet that somebody had lifted, then shaken, raising the earth and the trees as a wave passed beneath them. The ground started to vibrate wildly, knocking Frank off his feet.

"What was that?" Frank asked when the shaking stopped.

Joe looked up from where he was hugging the ground. "Where's Carlos?" he said.

"Here," their friend cried from below them. They crawled over to the ledge and looked down. Twelve feet down the face of the cliff, Carlos had landed on a ledge where a spiny bush prevented his falling farther.

"Are you okay?"

"I think so," he called up.

"Will the volcano blow?" Joe asked.

Frank said, "That was no volcano blast. Did you see that fireball? I'd say that was at least a twenty-millimeter charge."

Carlos was able to disentangle himself from the bush. He stood on a narrow ledge, brushing himself off. "Hey," he said. "This ledge is sort of like a path." He paused, then said, "I'll be right back." He inched along the ledge, then climbed down under the leaves of a tall tree that grew close to the cliff wall.

Joe said, "What kind of weapon was that?"

"I don't know for sure," Frank said. "But I think we just discovered where Tsotal lives."

Joe's eyes widened, and he began to nod his head. "I see. Earthquakes and cannons."

"And superstitions," Frank added.

"And sacrifices," Joe said. "I'm starting to smell a conspiracy."

Carlos returned to the ledge below them. "I found a cargo path," he said. "It probably leads down to where that explosion occurred."

"We should check this out," Joe said.

Frank looked at the sun. "Not much daylight left," he said. "What do you think, Carlos? How much time do we have left?"

"Perhaps an hour before sunset," he said. "If we don't hurry, we'll have to climb the volcano cone in the dark."

Joe said, "The sacrifice will happen at sunrise, is that right?" Carlos nodded. "How long does it take to climb the cone?"

"About three hours in daylight," Carlos replied. "I've never done it at night."

"We ought to check out this explosion," Frank said. "I suspect that these earthquakes are man-made. And I think I know what made them."

"Okay," Carlos said. "But we must hurry."

"We're with you, Carlos," Joe said. "Let's hustle." He lowered himself onto the ledge where Carlos stood, then followed him as he stepped into the limbs of the tree that brushed up against the cliff. They climbed down the tree trunk to the ground. At the foot of the tree, a rocky road cut a path over the twisted roots and tangled underbrush toward what they assumed was the site of the explosion.

As they descended into the vegetation, the leafy trees obscured the sky. With the last of the daylight now fading, the dark interior of the jungle reduced their visibility to about fifty feet. Shreds of ghostly mist hung listlessly in the air, and the ground under their feet became slimy with mud.

Carlos led the way. Frank could see his profile from time to time, and he could tell the young Ixilan was listening intently, using his ears as much as his eyes to probe the darkness ahead.

Off in the distance Joe could hear the strange cries of the night creatures emerging from their lairs, preparing themselves to begin their nocturnal hunt. He hurried to keep up with Frank, thinking that if a panther were stalking them, it might not attack a threesome.

Ahead, Carlos froze, listening. At first, Frank could hear only the cricketlike chirping of the insects, but then he caught the faint, steady clink of metal against metal—definitely a human sound.

Carlos moved more slowly now. Through the trees they soon saw some lights glimmering. Drawing closer, they positioned themselves behind a rock. In a clearing up ahead, several men were working around a giant cannon. Frank had never seen such a large weapon—it was about as big as a tractor trailer, but cylindrical. The giant barrel was held in place by hydraulic steel footings anchored to concrete slabs. The mouth of the cannon pointed toward the opposite side of the narrow valley.

The workers were dwarfed by its size. Each worker wore a miner's helmet with a built-in flashlight fixed to the crown. Frank could hear their voices calling and answering one another in Spanish.

"That's a scram-jet cannon," Frank told the others.

"There have been rumors that Micola was stockpiling weapons," Carlos said, "but I never thought he would go this far. What will he use it for?"

"Maybe just to intimidate people," Joe answered as they moved back deeper into the jungle and away from the cannon.

"He's definitely accomplished that," Frank said. "Remember how scared Leonora was by the earthquake? She truly believes that the death of Carlos's dad is the only way to stop it."

Carlos nodded, understanding Frank's logic. "So Micola will be the good guy by bringing my father to the people as a sacrificial lamb."

"Right," Frank said. "Micola accomplishes two things at once. He eliminates his rival el señor Capac *and* wins the support of the Ixilans in the elections."

Carlos shoved one fist into his other palm. "I will squash Micola!" he vowed.

Looking back toward the scram-jet cannon,

Frank said, "I don't like the size of this operation. Why don't we—"

He was cut off by the rustling of leaves nearby. Glancing over his shoulder, he was blinded by the piercing beam of a headlamp. He could not see the man's face behind the light, even by shielding his eyes, but lower down, poking into the circle of light, he did see a semiautomatic pistol—and the hand that held it. "Very clever, my young American friend," said the voice behind the light in a thick Spanish accent. "You found us. But I am more clever. I have found you."

Frank noticed with horror that the hand holding the gun had a ring on it, and on the ring was a wolf's head insignia.

Chapter

13

BECAUSE OF THE LIGHT in Joe's eyes, he could not see the man's face, but he recognized the voice.

Apparently Carlos did, too. "Umberto?" he said.

"Yes, *niño*," the man said. "We meet again. And this time you have no choice. You will either join my revolution or die."

"Wait a second—" Joe said.

"Shut up!" hissed the voice from behind the light. "You are a cockroach!"

"Easy," Frank said.

The voice was silent for a second. "Right you are, *americano*. Now is not the time to let one's passions rule one's head. Not with Micola's scram-jet fully operational."

That's right, keep talking, Joe said to himself, his eyes lowered to the ground, avoiding the bright light. Frank, he knew, was using the same tactic. If they avoided looking into the beam, their eyes would adjust to the dark more quickly once the light went out.

"That's an impressive weapon," Frank said, forcing his voice to remain steady. His hand crept to his back pocket, where Umberto could not see it. "What is Micola going to use it for?" Through the fabric of his jeans he felt the needle valve he had used back in Telos to unlock the handcuffs.

"Don't patronize me, *niño*," Umberto replied in a rough voice. "You wouldn't be following me if you didn't know what I had in mind. But I don't care. You're all too foolish to hide anything from me. The big, bad Network, so famous the world over, sends little boys to try to stop me! I spit on you Network spies!"

"Network?" Frank said. "We're not with the—"

"*¡Cállate!*" barked Umberto. "That innocent routine doesn't fool me. You already know of my plans. You know I'm not really one of Micola's men and that I plan to capture the scram-jet for my revolution. All you don't know is how. That's why you're sneaking around here."

Joe knew that Umberto was dangerous, but now he wondered if he also had a screw loose. "I hate to burst your bubble, pal," he said, "but we're not following you."

Umberto was silent, so Frank chimed in, "That's right. We're just trying to get to el señor Capac in time to stop the sacrifice."

"Your lies will not work," Umberto replied. "You have been following me since we were on the airplane together." He directed the beam to Carlos, and his voice changed, becoming softer. "If only you would have joined me."

"How did you know the Network was following you?" Frank asked.

"That man you work for—the one with the raincoat and the glasses—was following me," Umberto answered. "I lost him back in Soledad earlier today. So now he sends you, the American *niños,* to do his dirty work. And you have discovered the scram-jet cannon. How unfortunate for you."

Frank slowly moved his hand into the shadows behind his back. He was ready to flick the small metal valve back behind him. He hoped it would make a noise loud enough to distract Umberto. "I guess we'd better admit it, guys," Frank said, delaying his move a little longer. To Umberto he said, "We are with the Network, and we know all about your plan. There are Network SWAT teams all over this jungle."

The voice behind the light was silenced. Frank used this pause to flick the needle valve into the darkness behind him. He was lucky—it *pinged* off

118

a rock and skittered through some dry leaves. The light jerked up above them for a second.

It was all Joe needed. He launched himself forward, hitting Umberto's midsection. Umberto's gun fired, a bright flash and sharp crack in the night air, and his miner's hat flew off and rolled over the ground with its light still on.

Then Joe felt a hand grip his chin and force his head back. Swinging wildly, Joe slammed his fist into Umberto's solar plexus, and he felt the breath go out of his opponent.

Frank couldn't see a thing, but he heard Umberto grunt when Joe hit him. He quickly stepped toward the sound of the two bodies wrestling. A hand grazed his leg and Frank stepped on it blindly. Just as he stepped on the hand, the gun fired again, right under his foot! He kept his foot on Umberto's hand until he could remove the gun.

Breathing hard, Joe said, "So you thought you had us, huh?"

"Easy, Joe," Frank said. "Let's get him secured." Frank patted down the captive man and found a pair of handcuffs attached to his belt. They rolled Umberto over and cuffed his hands behind him. Frank retrieved the keys from Umberto's pocket, and the two brothers stood up.

They had heard shouting from the scram-jet area and could see lights bobbing among the trees, heading in their direction. Carlos whispered, "Let us go."

"We can't leave him here," Joe said. "They'll find him, and then he'll talk."

"We can't take him with us," Frank argued logically. "We don't have a choice."

Joe let out a frustrated sigh. "You're right," he said. "It's our only chance."

They slipped back the way they had come, deeper into the darkness, with Carlos leading the way. He had wonderful night vision. "Hold onto my belt," he whispered. "Joe, you hold on to Frank's."

Frank couldn't see a thing and frequently got slapped in the face by a branch overhanging the trail. Joe, too, kept brushing up against invisible things in the dark. At one point a spider's web draped across his face, and he impatiently slapped at it.

"Shhh," Frank warned him.

The lights and voices receded into silence, but still the boys kept moving. Heading uphill, they finally broke free of the oppressive vegetation. By now the moon had risen, and it cast an eerie light that bathed the rock cliffs above in inky black shadows.

They climbed onto the ridge and rested for a few moments, then resumed their journey to the top of the volcano. Each of them was thinking the same thing: Would they make it up the side of the cone before daybreak? Would they be able to stop the sacrifice?

They hiked slowly now, testing each step. The bright moon illuminated the rocks under their feet, but the light was tricky and sometimes cast shadows that fooled them, causing missteps. Joe concentrated on the narrow trail, but his mind was exploding with questions. "Frank?" he said.

"Quiet, little brother," Frank whispered.

"I've got to talk. If I don't, I'm going to go crazy."

"So talk," answered Frank from over his shoulder.

"Umberto said that the Network was following him," Joe said. "Do you think he was talking about the Gray Man?"

Frank thought about it for a second. "That would explain why you saw the Gray Man at the airport. He was following Umberto, not us."

They arrived at the place where the ridge met the smooth, nearly vertical cone of the volcano. Frank looked up at the smooth black wall— nearly vertical—that stretched above him for nearly four thousand feet. Carlos found a narrow crevasse that zigzagged up the steep rock face.

"These are the steps," Carlos said in a low voice. "I have never climbed them at night. We must be very careful." He started the ascent.

Frank followed him, feeling his way forward

with his feet. He encountered a step, then another above that.

"These must be ancient," he whispered to Carlos.

"Yes," Carlos replied. "They're called the stairway to heaven, and in ancient times my ancestors used them for all kinds of sacrifices in the volcano."

"How far up do they go?" Joe asked.

"All the way," Carlos said. "It'll take about three hours."

It was easy climbing at first. Joe concentrated on planting each foot squarely on the flat tread, then finding the next step before shifting his weight. As he got the hang of it, he looked around him. That was when he got scared. Behind him was the vast, open sky. They were over ten thousand feet up, far above the tree line.

He forced himself to concentrate on the steps and on Frank's back, swaying side to side as he climbed ever higher.

Before daybreak they reached the lip of the volcano. A deep cleft in the rim formed a kind of hallway providing access to the inside of the cone without climbing up to the highest peaks. Here Carlos paused. "There is shelter in here," he whispered. "But perhaps others are in there, too."

"How can we tell?" Frank whispered.

Joe peered into the narrow canyon. The moon

was no longer directly above them, so the passage-way was cast in black shadow. On part of the wall he did notice some deep carvings chiseled into the pumice, the same pattern as the tattoo on Carlos's arm.

Frank came up behind him. He spoke into his ear, "Let's stay out on the ledge for a while." Joe returned to where Carlos sat in a shallow depression in the rock wall. Frank volunteered to stay awake for a short watch while the others tried to get a little shut-eye.

Carlos and Joe sat leaning back against each other. Joe appreciated the extra warmth he felt radiating from Carlos. They looked out over the world in front of them—the distant curved horizon of the earth far away. It was the last sight Joe remembered before sleep overcame him.

When Joe woke up, Carlos was kneeling beside him, shaking him. "Come, quick," said his Ixilan friend. Joe saw Frank curled up beside him. Carlos had taken a second watch so Frank could sleep, too.

"Rise and shine," Joe said, shaking Frank.

The sun was almost up. The horizon glowed, and mist had formed over the foothills, clinging to the jungle below.

"Come with me quickly," Carlos urged again. He led them into the crevasse. Now Joe could see the full extent of the carvings on the rock walls. They were hieroglyphs of some kind, probably recounting great events in ancient Ixilan history. Joe didn't have a chance to linger over the carvings. He had to hurry through the rocky hallway. Twenty feet farther on, he abruptly emerged onto a ledge high up on the inside of the cone wall.

On this side of the cone, he saw a very different scene from the one he'd just left. A great dish-shaped, ash-covered valley was encircled by sheer rock walls—perhaps a mile across. Not a single piece of vegetation could be seen—just the even gray of smooth ash. Joe turned his nose up at the strong scent of rotten eggs. Sulphur, he thought.

Carlos was pointing over to their right. About a hundred yards away, on the same ridge on which they now stood, they saw a tent. Outside the tent, they saw a seated man tied to a stake driven into a crack in the rocks.

"It is my father," Carlos said simply.

Chapter
14

IN THE STILLNESS of the dawn, Joe heard the slow beat of a drum along with several chanting voices.

"Those are the Ixilan elders," Carlos whispered to Joe, pointing to the group of six men sitting in a semicircle around their prisoner. Joe noted their strange headgear and their ceremonial robes. One man wore a fierce hawk's head, with his own face appearing in the space of the open beak. Another wore a fantastic array of colorful parrot's feathers, arranged in a fan shape. A third wore the ears and fangs of a black panther. "They're singing the death prayer," Carlos said.

The ledge upon which Señor Capac was to be sacrificed was about twenty feet wide and perhaps forty feet long. There was a nylon tent anchored next to the wall of the cliff. Joe noticed with a chill that two armed guards, Micola's men, stood at attention outside the zipped flap of the tent.

"There's only one way off that ledge," Frank whispered. "They'll have to pass by us when they leave."

"But we can't wait until then," Carlos said tersely. "The sacrificial ceremony has already begun. We must act now."

"Do you want to walk into a bullet?" Frank asked. "What good would that do your father?" Carlos was silent, but Frank could tell that his silence wouldn't last long. The kid was ready to explode. "We do have surprise on our side," Frank added, "and shouldn't lose it."

Once again Joe peered around the rocky outcropping. The sun was nearly over the rim of the volcano. All of the Ixilan elders were now standing. They were still praying, but they had turned in unison to face the rising sun.

Just then a guard unzipped the tent flap. Two figures emerged, a man dressed in a military uniform and a woman wearing coveralls. Micola and Marta Capac!

They were talking to the guard. When Carlos saw them, he audibly groaned, then took off along the ledge. In a second he had reached full sprinting speed. Joe had just a moment to react before taking off after Carlos, with Frank right behind him. They knew it wasn't a good idea, but they didn't know what else to do.

The guard shouted, whipping his rifle up to his shoulder and aiming along the sight line. At the same time, Micola spun around, startled.

At that moment, Joe saw a few rocks above Micola's head loosen and tumble down. Then he felt the earth vibrate and surge under his feet. Suddenly he was running in the air, spinning his feet wildly. He came down hard, dangerously close to the rocky ledge.

Carlos, too, felt the surge of the earthquake, but his footing was sure, and he rode out the quake, skipping deftly over the rocks. The guard lost his footing, and fired high in the air.

The Ixilan elders scattered, leaving Señor Capac tied helplessly to the stake just two feet from the edge of the cliff.

It was the break Carlos needed. He launched himself into the air and tackled the guard with his full body weight. The gun went flying, skittering across the rocky flats and sailing off into the air over the edge. Joe was right behind him, hurling himself at the second guard.

Frank stepped in to help Carlos as he struggled with the first guard. From the corner of his eye he saw Micola grab Marta Capac's hand and dart back toward the passageway the Hardys had just left.

"I'll get them," Frank yelled, and he started to sprint back toward the passageway that led to the stairs. Before he got very far, he encountered the group of Ixilan elders. They surrounded him.

He could have beaten each of them easily, but together they formed too strong a unit and soon his arms were pinned. The hawk man gripped Frank's arms, while the man in the parrot's feathers held his feet.

Joe had just handcuffed the second guard when he saw that his brother was in trouble. He considered charging the group, but rejected the idea—there were six of them. After handcuffing the first guard, Carlos moved quickly to release his father. When Carlos untied his father's gag, the man smiled at his son. "I knew you'd come," said the elder Capac.

Joe could see that Carlos had Señor Capac's features—a wide forehead that gave him the appearance of intelligence, piercing black eyes, and a broad, flat nose. Unlike Carlos's, his hair was cut short and was streaked with gray.

With the Ixilan elders holding Frank, Joe wasn't sure if they would continue the sacrifice with Frank.

Apparently Señor Capac had the same thought because he glanced at the group of Ixilan elders as the last of his bonds fell away. "There will be no sacrifice today, gentlemen," he said in Spanish. His voice pierced the still morning air with the effect of a command. "Let the boy go."

"That's Frank," Carlos said, standing beside his father. "And his brother, Joe, over there. They helped me find you."

The Ixilan elder in the hawk's mask stepped away from those who held Frank. "You cannot escape your destiny, Capac," he said. "The old legends are clear. When Tsotal awakes, the king must die!" Carlos translated for Frank and Joe.

Señor Capac replied, "Tsotal? Where is he? Show me where he is, and I'll gladly jump in his mouth myself."

The hawk man answered by saying, "Can you deny the grumbling of Tsotal underneath your feet? That is proof enough that he is here."

"The mountainside does shake," Señor Capac responded. "And I cannot explain why—only scientists can do that. But I am sure that the earthquakes are not caused by Tsotal."

"We know only what the ancient stories tell us," said the hawk man. "To stop the mountain's quaking, we must sacrifice the king of the Ixilans. The old ways have worked before, and they will work again."

Carlos interrupted, shouting, "But my father's right! The mountain does not shake because of Tsotal. It is Micola who shakes the earth."

The hawk man laughed. "How can one little man like Micola shake a whole mountain, *niño?*"

"With his cannon," Carlos said.

Señor Capac turned to look at his son in surprise. "Micola has a cannon?"

"Yes, Father," Carlos replied. He described the scram-jet cannon, with its awesome, fire-belching power that shook the ground like an earthquake.

Frank confirmed Carlos's explanation. "We don't know what he plans to do with it, except to keep firing rounds at the volcano, causing all these earthquakes and destroying people's lives. But we have reason to believe that Umberto Corazón is planning to capture the cannon and use it against Micola.

At the mention of Umberto's name, Señor Capac frowned. "I never knew his organization was so powerful."

The Ixilan elders conferred among themselves. Finally they released their hold on Frank. The hawk man spoke again. "We wish to see this cannon. Until then, we cannot be sure what to believe."

"You are wise," Señor Capac said. "You will see that the days of sacrifice are over."

"Perhaps, Señor Capac," replied the hawk man. "But until the mountain no longer rumbles, we live in fear of our lives."

"We'll show you the cannon," Frank offered. "But Micola will probably get there first."

"Which means he'll be waiting for us," Joe added.

Carlos's face betrayed his worry. "And what of my aunt?" Nobody spoke for a moment, and Carlos's eyes filled with tears. "Please, somebody tell me why she was here!" Carlos could no longer translate, but Joe and Frank understood enough.

Señor Capac placed his hand on Carlos's shoulder. Joe could tell from his frown that the elder Capac was having difficulty forming his words. "Son, my sister has betrayed me, and she has lied to you. It wasn't until last night, when Micola brought her to the volcano to witness my execution, that I understood how completely—"

"I don't understand," Carlos interrupted. "She was in jail. She escaped with us."

"I know, my son," said Señor Capac. "But Micola guessed you would escape and you would trust her. Her orders were to keep an eye on you and to inform Micola if you got too close. She did her job admirably. She told me this when she arrived last night. Her words are still ringing in my ears, and my heart is sad."

"Traitor," Carlos said angrily. "We trusted her!"

"Yes, but she is my sister," said his father. "Perhaps we can still reason with her."

"How, Father?" said Carlos. "She lied to you and to me."

Señor Capac looked out over the bleak, gray, ash-covered valley, his dark eyes searching for an answer. "I don't know," he said. "But once we find her, we can ask her these questions."

The sun was high by the time the party had climbed slowly down the steps.

Joe was at the end of the line. The trail was so steep that it was like walking down a ladder—facing forward. He placed his feet carefully, testing each stone before putting his weight on it. In front of him, the two captured guards walked with their hands tied to their belts.

Frank walked ahead of the captives. He didn't like the situation one bit. On the vast wall of naked rock, they stood out boldly, easy targets for snipers from below.

He glanced down at the line of Ixilan elders in single file below him, led by Carlos and his father. Their progress in daylight was much easier, but Frank still couldn't keep up with them. At this rate, Frank figured they wouldn't pass the tree line for an hour.

Beyond the Ixilans, Frank could see the green rain forest canopy, draped over the sharp ridges and narrow valley of the volcano's foothills like a bunched-up carpet. He tried to identify the clearing where the scram-jet was located, but couldn't find it. He could see the scars, however, where the missiles had made contact with the mountain—burned-out pockets of scorched rock and destruction.

Then, as he gazed at the scene spread out below him, he saw the bright flash of an explosion but heard no sound. It was the cannon, but this time the missile rose straight up into the air, heading directly toward him, spewing flaming gas.

"Duck!" Frank cried, flattening himself into the thin crevasse and bracing himself against the narrow walls.

Chapter

15

AT FRANK'S WARNING, Joe jumped for cover and heard the speeding rocket whizz by. He felt the atmospheric pressure drop for a second and smelled the exhaust fumes a moment later. Luckily, the angle was too steep, and the missile flew past them, shooting high above the rim, leaving a white trail of smoke until it exploded.

For the first time the earth did not shake after the scram-jet gun was fired.

When it was safe to stand, Frank turned to Joe. "Come on," he urged. As quickly as he could, he climbed down the narrow path to join Señor Capac, Carlos, and the others.

When he reached the party of Ixilans, Frank heard an argument in progress, which Carlos translated for him. "In the name of the ancient warriors of our people, we will take revenge!" said the hawk man. "This man mocks our beliefs, he frightens the people, destroys our village with his false earthquakes." The other elders were nodding their heads in agreement.

Only Señor Capac disagreed. "Revenge is not the answer. Yes, he must be stopped, but we cannot kill him."

"How many has *he* killed?" replied the hawk man. "How many has he destroyed?"

"He will be brought to justice," Señor Capac said.

As they resumed their descent, Frank said to his brother at the rear of the line, "It's amazing how much respect Señor Capac has for the same people who, a couple of hours ago, were ready to toss him into the volcano. But he seems to trust them."

"I can see why Carlos admires his father so much," Joe said. "He didn't fly off the handle, in spite of all that's happened. And he isn't motivated by greed or revenge. He'd be a great president, if there actually would be fair elections. But somehow I doubt that Micola will ever play by the rules."

"Not as long as he has that scram-jet gun," Frank agreed. "What are we going to do about that?"

"Hope that he doesn't fire another one," Joe said.

"He won't," Frank guessed. "The angle is too steep. Even a smart bomb can't make a midair turn."

No sooner had he spoken than he was proven wrong. "Heads up!" Carlos said from the front of the line. They ducked again as another fire-spewing rocket rose from below. This one hit the mountainside a couple of hundred feet above them. Again, it didn't explode on contact, but shot off at a wild angle, spinning out of control. But the consequences of the brush with the mountain were still serious.

Joe saw the avalanche coming. "Everybody stay down," he shouted to the group below him. The cascade of rocks was brief and loud, sounding like thunder but feeling like another earthquake. Because the crevasse in which they were hidden was so narrow, few of the rocks were channeled into it. The climbing party escaped injury by pressing themselves into the narrow crevasse while the avalanche passed over them.

Frank was the first to pop his head up over the edge of the crevasse. "They're probably reloading," he said.

Joe said, "That gives us maybe ten minutes, right?"

"I don't know," Frank said. "But I'm not waiting around to find out. Let's go!"

Crouching now and moving faster than before, the party continued downward. Finally they reached the end of the steps, the place where the ridge met the upper cone of the volcano.

Frank expected to meet Micola's men at this juncture, but the area around the bottom of the steps was deserted. They conferred about what to do.

"We should keep moving," Frank said, eyeing the ridge ahead of them, with its sharp cliffs falling away on each side. He knew the group would be exposed as long as they were on it. "Carlos, do you think you can find that trail again?"

"Most certainly," Carlos said.

"What will we do when we get there?" Señor Capac asked.

"There are ten of us," the hawk man said.

"There were at least ten of Micola's men working at the scram-jet site," Frank said. "Probably more."

"What should we do with these guys?" Joe asked, dangling a set of handcuff keys from the end of his finger and jerking his head over to the uniformed guards.

"We can't take them with us," Frank said.

The hawk man said, "Leave them here. We will come back for them tonight."

It didn't take Carlos long to find the trail they had discovered the night before. With Carlos leading, they began to creep down toward the scram-jet site.

"Something is very wrong," Frank whispered as he followed Joe along the path. "First they are firing at us as if they want to annihilate us, and now that we're closing in, they don't seem to care."

Carlos was scouting ahead. He came back to them, breathless. "Look," he said, pointing up. Through a break in the trees they saw a black plume of smoke rising.

Then they heard gunshots in the woods. The chatter of a machine gun was punctuated by the crack of a high-powered rifle.

Frank waved to the rest to stay behind. He joined Carlos and Joe as they crept through the underbrush until they got close enough to see into the camp. The cannon was now raised into an upright position. At its base was an overturned cargo truck. One of *los lobos* was hiding behind it. Just after Frank identified the man as Umberto, the truck burst into flames. Umberto was shielded from the fire by the truck's spilled cargo—several crates of metal canisters that must have broken open when the truck was overturned. Now the crates were starting to catch fire.

"Uh-oh," Joe said. "That's our pal Umberto down there. Micola's men must have found him and set him free. My guess is that he's started to make his move. He's actually trying to start a revolution here and now and by himself."

Frank noticed that the fire was starting to spread. Already it had engulfed one of the methane gas canisters. "Umberto is going to be dead if one of those canisters blows," Frank observed.

"Micola's machine gun is over there," Joe said, pointing to a thicket off to their right at the edge of the clearing. Umberto apparently thought so, too, because he peered over the edge of a crate and fired into the thicket where Frank was pointing. "We could probably sneak behind Micola's men and surprise them."

"No way," Carlos said. "Let Umberto deal with his own mistakes—he's one lone man. We're going after Micola and Marta Capac."

"I doubt they're anywhere near here," Joe said. "Maybe Umberto took care of them."

"We can't stay here," Frank said. Crouching, the boys took advantage of another burst of gunfire to cover their retreat back to Señor Capac and the Ixilan elders.

"Umberto has started his revolution," Carlos told his father.

"Maybe we ought to try to neutralize it," Frank said.

"I said forget Umberto," Carlos said angrily. "It's Micola we want."

Joe said, "I'm sure they hightailed it out of there when Umberto started his shooting spree."

"Listen," Frank said to Carlos. "Umberto and his underground could probably make a good guess about where Micola and Marta Capac went, right?" Carlos nodded. "If we don't do something to rescue Umberto, then he may blow up with all those methane gas canisters and he'd never be able to tell us where Micola went. Now, are you with me?"

Slowly Carlos nodded again, and the others stood close to hear Frank's plan as Carlos translated it. Frank demonstrated a low whistle. "When you hear that sound, it means Joe, Carlos, and I have neutralized that machine gun. That's your signal to fan out behind Umberto. When he realizes the machine gun is out, he's going to try to bolt."

Joe led the way, with Frank and Carlos following closely behind as they headed for the thicket. The Ixilans and Carlos's father crept toward the clearing where Umberto was pinned down. Sporadic bursts of gunfire kept the boys aware of their position in relation to the thicket. The jungle around the camp was thick with dense undergrowth and rotting leaves, so they stepped very lightly and kept a good distance from the machine gun.

Finally they sneaked up behind the thicket. Joe could see two men in *los lobos* uniforms about twenty yards away, shielding themselves from Umberto's fire with a fallen tree trunk. Joe guessed the other *lobos* had retreated with Micola and Marta Capac.

Silently Carlos crept forward, ahead of Joe, positioning himself fifteen feet away. Frank joined him. Silence was crucial. Joe held back, watching his brother and Carlos signal to each other. They were crouched and ready. The next time the machine gun started to chatter, they made their move.

Joe, too, darted forward, ready to cover for them in case one of the guards made a break for it. Frank and Carlos landed simultaneously on the backs of the gunners, surprising them. One of them managed to yell loudly before Frank could silence him with a right hook. By then Joe had arrived to help, and the three quickly disarmed them. Frank whistled.

In the silence that followed, the boys all listened for any other sound. Without warning a huge explosion rocked the clearing. Flaming debris rained down around them in the seconds following the blast.

Frank was the first to raise his head, and what he saw made him shout, "Stay down!" Above their heads, the giant barrel of the cannon was tilting dangerously. It was starting to fall.

Chapter

16

WITH A SHRIEK OF TEARING METAL, the barrel of the scram-jet cannon tore free from its hydraulic supports and fell down on top of the overturned truck. The crash shook the earth under Frank's body.

The crash had literally extinguished the fire by scattering the crates and unexploded canisters of methane gas to the edges of the clearing. On the far side of the fallen cannon Frank found the Ixilans holding Umberto captive.

Umberto had a gash on his cheek and his face was blackened with carbon and dirt. "Ah, the Network *niños,*" he said. "I might have known."

Ignoring him, Frank said, "We've got to secure this area. No telling who heard that crash, but chances are they'll come back to find out what it was. And we need to be ready for them."

"I want to question Umberto," Carlos said, "so I will stay here."

"I'll stay with you," Frank said. "In fact, we should all buddy up—a solo search would be dangerous."

"I'll do a sweep back there," Joe said, pointing back toward the thicket where the two snipers were secured.

"I'll go with Joe," Señor Capac said. "The rest of you, search the cargo trail and fan out on the far side of the clearing." As the Ixilan elders were pairing off, Señor Capac added, "Two of you should bring back the men we left at the ridge."

Frank and Carlos took cover with Umberto in the cement bunker behind the scram-jet cannon. It was a low-ceilinged room, built of reinforced cement walls, designed to withstand the enormous kickback that resulted from a missile firing.

After making sure none of Micola's guards were hiding inside, Frank inspected the electronic circuitry of the scram-jet's control panel. He couldn't understand all of the dials and levers, but he did know that someone had taken a machine gun to it. Bullet holes punctured the control panel, smashing glass and exposing the blackened wires underneath.

"I did that," Umberto said, following Frank's gaze.

"Just tell us where Micola and Marta Capac are," Carlos said. "And do not waste time."

"They are gone," Umberto said. "In a truck. They're probably in Soledad by now." His voice grew angry. "He was right here, aiming the scram-jet up at you on the volcano cone. I couldn't let him do that. So I took a machine gun and destroyed the controls before he could do any more mischief. He escaped from me at that time and took Marta Capac with him. I tried to catch them, but that is when the truck overturned."

"Is there another vehicle?" Carlos asked.

Umberto shook his head. Carlos looked at Frank. "We must get down to Soledad."

Frank didn't see how. "It's a long hike, Carlos," he said.

They were interrupted by Joe and Carlos's father, leading the two snipers. "The area's secure," Joe reported. "Looks like Micola's police have disappeared for good. I posted the others on lookout duty. What did you find out here?"

"Micola and Marta Capac took a truck down to Soledad," Frank said.

Señor Capac said, "It is a shame. But how much more damage can they do?" He glanced out the door toward the disabled scram-jet cannon. "Once I expose Micola's secret weapon and explain the earthquakes, the people of Payumac will never vote for him again."

"Elections, ha!" said Umberto. "You think elections will stand in the way of a black-hearted villain like Micola? Don't you see how evil he is?"

"Yes, my friend," Señor Capac said. "I do. And so will the voters."

"No!" Umberto said. "He can only be stopped by killing him and destroying his headquarters."

"What will that prove?" Señor Capac asked.

"That evil can be destroyed," Umberto answered. "It will prove that Micola's brand of power is wrong. It will prove that his neglect of the native people of Payumac has consequences."

"But will you replace him with a better kind of power?" Señor Capac asked. "Killing will always be killing, no matter who does it. And a murderer can never lead Payumac."

Umberto seemed to be listening to Señor Capac. "I haven't murdered yet," he admitted. "But I have tried."

"Yes, I know," Señor Capac said. "But things must change."

They were interrupted by one of the elders, who slipped into the bunker quietly. "Someone is coming," he said. A second later they all heard a vehicle approaching. Frank ducked out the door, and Joe followed.

The two brothers took a position behind the

fallen cannon, peering over it at the cargo trail. Two four-wheel-drive personnel carriers appeared through the trees. On the doors of the vehicles, Frank could see the now-familiar wolf's head insignias of Micola's *los lobos*.

"If that's Micola," Frank said, "he found reinforcements." To himself he added, And there are twice as many of them as there are of us.

Through the windshield of the lead truck, Frank recognized two faces—those of Micola and Marta Capac. But a third person was driving the truck. The Gray Man! The trucks pulled to a halt in front of the fallen cannon. The Gray Man got out, along with Micola and Marta Capac. When Frank saw the two fugitives in handcuffs, he stepped out into the open. He was so surprised that he just stood and stared. Joe let out a whoop of recognition and ran out to the trucks, leaping and shouting at the top of his lungs. The Gray Man acted slightly uncomfortable during this reception, but he managed a grin finally.

"What are you doing here?" Joe asked.

"I ran into these two," said the Gray Man, gesturing toward the captive pair. By now, what Joe assumed were Network operatives in camouflage fatigues had disembarked from the back of the canvas-covered trucks. The Gray Man continued, "So I borrowed a couple of Micola's trucks and persuaded him to bring me here."

Micola was gazing in horror at the fallen

scram-jet cannon. "It is destroyed," he said, fixing his coal dark eyes on Señor Capac, who had emerged from the bunker accompanied by his son.

"The tables have turned," Capac said to the pair.

"Perhaps for now, Capac," Micola growled. "But *los lobos* will not disappear so easily."

The Gray Man interrupted. "Think again, Micola. Once they saw that we had captured you, they seemed pretty willing to help us. My men are negotiating with them right now to secure the airport, and pretty soon they'll be laying down their weapons."

Señor Capac gestured to the small group of Ixilan elders, who had abandoned their lookout posts and gathered around the trucks. "It seems your wolves have not destroyed the true Ixilan spirits—the men who hold the old ways of our country strong in their hearts and actions."

"Señor Capac," the Gray Man said, "if I could have just a moment of your time?" All eyes turned toward the Network operative. He adjusted his glasses and said, "I suggest, sir, that—" He hesitated. "What I mean to say, sir, is that this weapon"—he gestured to the massive cannon in the clearing—"is a matter of utmost international importance."

"Yes?" Señor Capac said.

"And I would like to offer to secure this area with some of my men."

"Of course," Señor Capac said.

The Gray Man spoke to one of the Network operatives, who began to set up a headquarters. All the while Señor Capac had stood gazing steadily at Marta Capac.

She did not hang her head, as Joe would have expected. Instead, she met her brother's gaze with a defiantly uplifted chin. Joe had to admire her, even though he knew now that she was a traitor. He wondered what had possessed the woman to turn on her own brother and operate as a spy for Micola.

"What have you to say for yourself, sister?" Señor Capac demanded. His voice was steady, but Frank could tell that he was deeply troubled.

"Only that I hope you have the same kind of luck in running Payumac as you had in surviving the sacrifice."

"It was your idea then," said her brother, "to exploit the people's superstitions by creating the earthquakes. Only you could have known how quickly they would revert back to the old ways."

"Yes," she said. "And it would have worked, if not for Carlos's efforts. And those of his friends."

"You seem to have no remorse," Capac observed.

"Remorse? For what?" she replied. "You don't understand the Payumac people. They need discipline, not freedom. You want to take all that

Micola has built and give it over to the people, but they won't know what to do with it." She paused, and for the first time Joe heard a note of bitter disappointment in her voice. "You would have lost the elections," she said.

Micola looked at Marta Capac and said, "When I get out of this, I'll reward your loyalty."

"I don't think you'll be getting out of anything very soon," Señor Capac said. "Either of you. For now, you'll go to jail. And if I am elected, I'll make sure there is a trial."

The Gray Man joined the group again. "We should get back to Soledad," he said. "My men have set up a communications center so we'll be able to call in reinforcements from Telos."

The group broke up, with the Ixilans climbing in the back of one truck, guarding Micola and Marta Capac. Carlos joined Frank, Joe, and the Gray Man in the cab, while Señor Capac drove the other truck along with the captain of the Network operatives.

Bouncing along the unpaved trail through the valley, Frank and Joe finally got to question the Gray Man. They started together—and at once. Joe won out and wanted to know why the Gray man had been at the airport.

"I was tailing Umberto," he explained. "We knew he was planning to stage a revolution against Micola by stealing the scram-jet, but we didn't know where it was. We thought Umberto would lead us to it, but he slipped away. We lost him in Soledad, but knew we were close to the scram-jet cannon. Without Umberto we didn't know how to find it—at least not until Micola led us to it."

"How much farther to Soledad?" Joe asked.

"About another mile or so," Carlos replied. "That is, what's left of it," he added glumly.

"The damage is pretty extensive," the Gray Man remarked.

Carlos said angrily, "Micola will pay for this destruction. I will make sure of it."

"Can we make a telephone call from there?" Frank asked. "Joe and I should check in with our dad and mom to let them know we're all right."

"And my mother," Carlos added. "She will be overjoyed to hear that my father is safe."

As the truck rumbled into the outskirts of the city, Joe could see a half-collapsed house nestled among the trees. "I guess there'll be a lot of clean-up work."

The Gray Man nodded. "We've already sent word to the Red Cross and other international relief organizations. They'll arrive later today to set up medical stations and food camps."

Carlos said to Frank and Joe, "I hope you can stay for a few days. I think we'll need your help."

"I doubt that our parents would go for it," Frank said. "Besides, we've already missed most of a week of soccer camp back in Bayport."

Joe clapped his hand to his forehead. "That's right! I almost forgot." Then he groaned. "Coach Jordan is going to kill us."

Frank said, "Especially when he learns that Carlos isn't coming back."

Joe and Frank looked soberly at their friend. "I am sorry," Carlos said. "But I belong here with my father and my mother."

"It looks like Bayport is losing its best soccer player," Frank commented.

"I am afraid so," Carlos replied without modesty, then grinned. "But I'll come back to visit you sometime soon. Maybe I will even be able to join the team in a game."

"Cool," Joe said. "Just don't let the coach catch you without shoes."

Frank and Joe's next case:

Frank and Joe stroll out of the movies straight into a real-life drama in progress: a lightning-quick bank robbery. Guns blazing, bullets flying, the same masked gang has hit a batch of local banks, always pulling off the heist right after the arrival of a new shipment of cash. But now the Hardys are in the hunt, vowing to make the robbers pay. Cutting them down won't be easy, though. Not only have the crooks crafted near-perfect disguises, they're loaded with firepower and ready to let it fly. But the boys have come up with one lead from a very surprising source: Joe's girlfriend, Vanessa. The clue could turn the case in the Hardys' favor . . . if the gang doesn't turn on Vanessa first . . . in *Wrong Side of the Law,* Case #102 in The Hardy Boys Casefiles™.